why i let my hair
grow out

Maryrose Wood

BERKLEY JAM, NEW YORK

THE BERKLEY PUBLISHING GROUP
Published by the Penguin Group
Penguin Group (USA) Inc.
375 Hudson Street, New York, New York 10014, USA
Penguin Group (Canada), 90 Eglinton Avenue East, Suite 700, Toronto, Ontario M4P 2Y3, Canada
(a division of Pearson Penguin Canada Inc.)
Penguin Books Ltd., 80 Strand, London WC2R 0RL, England
Penguin Group Ireland, 25 St. Stephen's Green, Dublin 2, Ireland (a division of Penguin Books Ltd.)
Penguin Group (Australia), 250 Camberwell Road, Camberwell, Victoria 3124, Australia
(a division of Pearson Australia Group Pty. Ltd.)
Penguin Books India Pvt. Ltd., 11 Community Centre, Panchsheel Park, New Delhi—110 017, India
Penguin Group (NZ), 67 Apollo Drive, Mairangi Bay, Auckland 1311, New Zealand
(a division of Pearson New Zealand Ltd.)
Penguin Books (South Africa) (Pty.) Ltd., 24 Sturdee Avenue, Rosebank, Johannesburg 2196,
South Africa

Penguin Books Ltd., Registered Offices: 80 Strand, London WC2R 0RL, England

This book is an original publication of The Berkley Publishing Group.

This is a work of fiction. Names, characters, places, and incidents either are the product of the author's imagination or are used fictitiously, and any resemblance to actual persons, living or dead, business establishments, events, or locales is entirely coincidental. The publisher does not have any control over and does not assume any responsibility for author or third party websites or their content.

PRINTING HISTORY
Berkley JAM trade paperback edition / March 2007

Library of Congress Cataloging-in-Publication Data

Wood, Maryrose.
    Why I let my hair grow out / Maryrose Wood. — Berkley Jam trade pbk. ed.
        p. cm.
    Summary: On a bike trip in Ireland trying to recover from a broken heart, sixteen-year-old Morgan is transformed, not only by the others on the tour, but by her visits to the past, where she is believed to be the legendary half-goddess Morganne, sent to help end a faery curse.
    ISBN 978-0-425-21380-3 (trade pbk.)
    [1. Bicycle touring—Fiction. 2. Interpersonal relations—Fiction. 3. Time travel—Fiction. 4. Fairies—Fiction. 5. Self-esteem—Fiction. 6. Ireland—Fiction.] I. Title.

    PZ7.W8524Why 2007
    [Fic]—dc22
                    2006033506

PRINTED IN THE UNITED STATES OF AMERICA

10 9 8 7 6 5 4 3 2 1

For my mom, Rita,
who is definitely at least half goddess.
And for my dad, Eddie,
who would have enjoyed a trip to Ireland.

acknowledgments

Writing this book was a pleasure from start to finish, and that is due to the witty and wise stewardship of editor Jessica Wade. Much appreciation to the copyediting genius Jenny Brown, and to Sarah Howell, Monica Benalcazar, and Rita Frangie for the wild and magical cover art.

A tad irreverently, *Why I Let My Hair Grow Out* references characters and incidents from the rich tradition of Irish mythology. I encourage any interested readers to dive into this material; it's vastly entertaining and you'll love it. There are many marvelous retellings of the legend of Cúchulainn; I especially recommend Rosemary Sutcliff's *The Hound of Ulster*. For more suggested readings (as well as a playlist of some truly shamrockin' Irish music) please visit www.maryrosewood.com.

Hurling is an ancient sport that is still played with passion and enjoyment by athletes all over the world. To learn more, visit the website of the Gaelic Athletic Association (GAA) at www.gaa.ie.

As always, I'm grateful for the savvy guidance and unfailing encouragement provided by my agent, Elizabeth Kaplan, and my dear friend Emily Jenkins.

Thanks to the late, legendary editor Leona Nevler, who acquired this book for Berkley. I deeply regret that we never had the chance to meet.

one

the first thing i did was take scissors to my bangs. *Snip, snip.* Or maybe I should say, *bang, bang.* My heart was beating kind of hard.

It looked okay. The hair formerly-known-as-bangs was sticking up and out, like the brim of a baseball cap that was tilted way back on my head. Too jaunty for my current state of mind, though. I picked up the scissors again.

Snip, snip. You never realize how long your hair is till you chop off a piece right next to your scalp, smooth it out and hold it in your hands. That was a good two feet of hair lying there. Dark, except for the roots. My hair is naturally a pale reddish-blond color. My mom used to call it "strawberry blond" with this kind of pride, like, *Smell me, I have a kid with strawberry-blond hair*. I put an end to that crap in January when I started dying it black.

Chop. Chop. Chop. Some things are hard to stop, once you begin. *Chop.*

When it was all over, and I looked at what I had done, I was pleased.

from October to june, raphael had been drawing a map of me, but everything was in the wrong place. That's how it felt. Raphael patted my skinny ass and made remarks about my big booty. He found it amusing to introduce me as "Morgan, my girlfriend who has no sense of humor," but my friends (back when I used to have friends) always thought I was the funny one.

Raphael looked at my favorite *New Yorker* cartoons and didn't "get" them. He called me sweet when I was trying to sound mad. He met my family and found them "perfectly nice" and "too sentimental," when it was obvious that both my parents were control freaks and my little sister was a battery-operated robot girl who'd been programmed by Disney.

If Raphael described me to you, you would never know it was me. If you took his map of me and tried to find your way from my nose to my chin, you'd get lost before you got past the nostril.

The thing is, after exactly one school year minus one month of going out with Raphael, I started to think maybe his map was right, and mine was wrong.

And then he broke up with me, and I didn't have a map left at all.

* * *

the look on my mother's face when she saw my hair was an amazing thing to behold.

"Morgan—" she said. Her eyes got all wet looking and she covered her mouth with her hands. "Oh, my. I wish—I wish you'd—" She stopped, and her car keys slipped from her fingers to the kitchen floor.

"Time for a change," I said.

I knew what she was thinking. She was thinking that I was taking the Raph breakup way too hard and acting like a huge drama queen and doing stupid crap with my hair to get attention and sympathy and whatever. It was such a waste of breath for my mom to say nice things to me, because I always knew what she was really thinking and it was never the same as what she said.

"Yes." She picked up her keys and didn't look at me. "A change, yes. And you have such a beautiful face, you look great with short hair."

Obviously I had not gone far enough.

"Stripes!" tammy screamed, when i got in the car. "Orange stripes! Morgan looks like a clown!"

"Buckle up, Tam."

"Mommy, did you see what Morgan did to her hair? She put stripes in it!"

"Yes, Tam. Did you buckle?"

"And she doesn't hardly even have any hair left! It's just— fuzz. Fuzz with orange stripes!"

"Morgan, would you please buckle your sister?"

Seven years old and the brat couldn't work her own seat

belt. I yanked the belt too hard as I roped her in. "If we're in a head-on collision and this saves your life, you'll owe me forever," I said with a growl.

"Shut up, *clowny*."

"No calling names, Tammy," Mom said, checking her lipstick in the mirror. "Hurting names hurt people, just like hitting hurts people."

"You know what really hurts people?" I whispered in Tammy's ear. "When you're in a car and it plunges off a bridge into the water and you can't get your seat belt open, and there's water pouring in all the vents and windows and you're trapped and you know you're gonna drown and there's nothing you can do about it, all because of your goddam seat belt."

"MOM!" Tammy started crying like the baby she was. "Make her stop!"

"Stop what, Tam?"

"Stop being *evil*! I hate her! Why do I have to have the worst sister of anyone?"

Mom sighed and said nothing and pulled out onto the road. I sat back, contented. Tammy's misery was especially satisfactory because we were on our way to Lucky Lou's, and Tammy always loved going to Lucky Lou's.

Lucky Lou's is an enormous grocery store, known far and wide in the state of Connecticut for its commitment to obscene overkill of every kind. The food is piled in enormous, towering, wasteful heaps, in cruel mockery of all those third-world countries where people are actually starving. In each aisle there's a grinning Lucky Lou employee who trails your every step, trying to help you find stuff in this pushy, phony way.

Sadly, Lucky Lou's real claim to fame is that inside the store there are dozens of freak-show mechanical figures crammed in every corner, on the tops of the shelves and hung from the ceiling. There are zucchini and cucumbers and tomatoes dressed in farmer outfits, chickens in little bonnets and leering, wide-eyed cartons of orange juice and eggs, plus a life-size, horrifying cow, all lurching and waving their rusty limbs and screeching tinny songs about the goodness of milk and vegetables and the supreme magnificence of Lucky Lou's.

Lucky who? Lucky you!
Shopping here at Lucky Lou's!

Tammy would dance around the store singing along with this crap, providing even more proof of her battery-operated robot-girl status. But now she was too upset to have fun, and that was my doing. Lucky who? Lucky me.

My friend Sarah and I (this is back when i had friends, which was before I started going out with Raphael), we used to play this game called "Name a Connecticut Town." There are three lists of words and you take one from each, and it always makes the name of a Connecticut town. The first list is words like:

North

South

East

West

Old

And the second is:

Nor

Green

Port

Stam

Mill

And the third is:

Haven

Walk

Chester

Ford

Which

It totally works. Everyone in Connecticut lives in a town called South Norford or East Greenwalk or West Porthaven or Old Stamwich. That's where my family lived too. A Connecticut town, not far from Lucky Lou's, in which Raphael was no longer my boyfriend. Pick any name you like or in-

vent your own. It really doesn't matter. Maps are only paper,
anyway.

"i hate you i hate you i hate you." tammy sobbed,
kicking the back of the driver's seat. Mom asked her to stop
but she acted like she didn't hear. Clearly this would be the
longest trip to Lucky Lou's ever. I didn't care. Mom had insisted I come along, I think because after the hair incident she
was afraid to leave me alone in the house even for half an hour.

I ran my hand over my nearly naked head, with its scream-
ing orange streaks in the two-tone stubble. *Time for a change.*
That's what Raphael had said to me two weeks ago, in late
June, on the last day of school.

"Time for a change, Morgan." He wasn't looking at me;
he was looking at the vending machine that stood between
the locker room entrances by the gym, trying to decide which
candy to buy. Boys on one side, girls on the other, candy in
the middle. It's the kind of thing Sarah and I would have
wanted to interpret, finding a symbolic and hilarious meaning in the placement of the vending machine. If I'd said
something like that to Raph, he'd point out that that's where
the electrical outlet was.

Just get the Twizzlers, I thought as I watched him. *You always get those. Don't shop around for something better or the
Twizzlers will feel really bad.* He jingled some change in his
hand. "You know I'm going to camp for, like, practically all
of July and August."

"Yeah," I said. Some part of me understood right away
where this was headed but I thought I could fight it. "You'll

have a great time." Raph was very smart and good at every-thing, and he'd gotten accepted to an elite gifted-leaders-of-tomorrow camp at M.I. frikkin' T. That would be his summer of love. Raph and the gifted leaders of tomorrow. No surfer-dude he, no slacker, not Raph.

"I'm gonna be a senior next year," he said. Like I'd forgotten how old he was.

"Look, they restocked the Butterfingers," I said. If I acted like I didn't get it, I could buy myself some time. That was a favorite strategy of mine when under pressure. Stall, play dumb, grab another precious thirty seconds of happiness before my world came crashing down.

"Do you get what I'm saying?" Raph punched in the code for his candy and started talking louder, like I was deaf. "I'm gonna be away all summer, and next year is my last year before college, and I just think we could both use a change."

Raph always knew what was best for me.

"I don't want a change." My voice sounded small.

He scooped a Twix bar out of the machine and kept talking as if I hadn't said anything.

"It was fun going out with you this year. We had some fun, right? You'll have a great summer, Morgan. You'll meet people and, whatever."

I knew what he was thinking. He was thinking I was too young for him, too boring, too dim to keep up with that sharp-witted brainiac banter he and his friends traded all the time. He was tired of explaining his physics homework to me and me not getting it. He probably wanted a whiz-kid girl-friend, some glossy, fast-talking, put-together girl like the girls he'd meet at camp, a girl who'd run for student council president next year and let him manage her campaign.

Raph would be good at that. Raph liked to pull strings from behind the scenes, and he was very concerned with people's "images." He would sometimes tell me that my "image" needed work. I never knew what he meant by it, except that obviously he was somehow disappointed in me. It had been his idea that I dye my hair dark, so I'd have more of an "edge."

All I ever noticed about people's "images" was how different they acted compared to what they were really thinking. For some reason, I could always tell what people were really thinking.

Time for a change, Raph was saying. But what he was really thinking was, *I tried and tried to make you into a girlfriend who would be interesting to me, and it didn't work. I guess you just don't have what it takes.*

In the rest of Connecticut two weeks had passed since we broke up, but in my own personal space-time continuum I was still standing there on the last day of school, watching Raph unwrap his Twix bar while his unspoken words took up permanent residence in my brain. They were loud and constant, like the crash of waves on a beach.

I did my best, but you just couldn't cut it, Morgan. That's why it's time for a change.

It was hard to hear anything else.

Case in point: Tammy was still sitting in the back seat next to me, crying, but I didn't hear her at all.

two

i stared at the shiny travel brochure my dad had handed me and all I could think of was the game I used to play with Sarah: *Come on, everybody! Let's play Name an Irish Town! Killarney and Kenmare and West Cork and, excuse me, Dingle.*

"So you see, kiddo, it's all set. It's a week-long tour. You'll have a blast."

I still couldn't believe there was a town named Dingle, but there it was, right on the map. I wasn't paying too much attention to my dad at that point. Just staring at Dingle.

"So whaddya say? Sounds exciting, right?"

Dingle dingle dingle.

"Morgan?"

"Sorry, what?" If I pretended I didn't get it, I could buy myself some time. A brilliant strategy that had been working so frikkin' well for me in my life so far.

"I said, what do you think? About the trip?"

"Um, yeah," I said. "I think I missed what you said. I'm getting a new bike or something?"

Mom was buzzing and whirring around the kitchen while Dad and I were having this delightful little talk, and I could tell what she was thinking from the careless way she emptied the dishwasher. "Why?" wailed the salad plates, as they clattered together in the cabinets. "Why did my firstborn child turn out to be such a loser?"

Stupid for her to pretend she wasn't eavesdropping, anyway, since you can't *not* eavesdrop in my house. Mom and Dad were dumb enough to buy one of those "open plan" houses, where the kitchen is part of the dining room and the dining room is part of the living room, and when Tammy puts on her frikkin' educational TV programs the whole house is one big Discovery Channel.

I'd sworn to myself a thousand times: When I grow up I'm going to have a house with rooms. With doors. That *close*.

Dad had spent far less time with me over the last sixteen years than Mom had, due to his working like a slave to pay for our fabulous open-plan house in North No-name, Connecticut. So he never developed Mom's psychic ability to know right away when I was yanking the parental chain.

Poor Dad. He took the brochure out of my hands and turned the pages for me, slowly, like it was story time in preschool.

"It's a bike tour, see? They give you a bike when you get there, and there's a tour guide and a van that drives along behind to carry your luggage or give you a ride if you get tired. And you get to ride your bike through all this beautiful Irish countryside. Can you believe these pictures, huh? Look how green the grass is!"

"No offense, Dad, but you and Mom haven't ridden bikes in years. And Tammy's just gonna whine the whole way. Did you consider Club Med at all?" Dad looked annoyed all of a sudden, but I didn't know why. I was just trying to participate and help plan the family vacation. Wasn't that what we were doing?

I heard a tense, warning jangle of silverware from the kitchen portion of the room. "The trip is for you, Morgan," Dad said, sounding gruff. "Your mom and I, we think you've had a tough year. And sometimes a vacation is a good thing. Mentally, I mean." Then he shut up. Whenever my dad gets out of his element, he clams up and waits for my mom to take over.

Cue Mom, who didn't even bother to pretend she hadn't been listening. "What your father is trying to say is, we both feel you need a break." Mom emerged from behind the "kitchen island" with her hands on her hips. She always calls it the "kitchen island," like it has palm trees growing out of it. *Hello, it's a countertop, Mom.* "A change, you said so yourself. We've been, frankly, a little worried."

"I'm fine, Mom." My eyes started to roll on their own, but when I realized I was doing it, I exaggerated it, just for the effect.

"I hope so, Morgan. But there has been some behavior lately, some *extreme* behavior. . . ."

"You mean, like, my hair?" I'd been waiting for this moment. Looking forward to it, in fact.

"Yes, that's one thing—"

"Wait," I said. Time to turn up my attitude. "*Wait*. You want me, by myself, to go ride a bike across a foreign country with towns named *Dingle,* just because I cut my *hair*? Isn't *that* a little extreme?"

"You won't be by yourself. It's a group tour. There will be all kinds of people." Mom faked a smile. "It'll be fun."

"So *you* go, if it's so frikkin' fun! I'll stay home."

"Watch the language, Morgan." Language patrol was definitely Dad's element. Good to know he was still listening.

Mom dropped the smile and crossed her arms, and now she did not look very fun loving at all. "Let's talk about Raphael," she said.

"No. Way." I got up. One lousy door to slam behind me, that's all I needed, and there was none to be found.

"Morgan! We're trying to help you! You've been acting like, like—"

"A total bitch?" I sneered. Gotta throw Dad a bone now and then; it keeps him involved.

"Morgan!" he boomed. "What did I say about language?"

"Forget it, Daniel." She turned back to me. "Yes, in fact! Since you and Raphael broke up, you have been acting very mean and hurtful, to us, to Tammy, and most importantly, to yourself."

Oh, please. "It's just *hair*!" I said, in my most mean and hurtful tone. "And it's *my* hair. Anyway, it has nothing to do with you or Dad or Tammy or"—for some reason it was hard to say Raph's name—"or anybody!"

Mom was on a rescue mission now, though. There was no stopping her with logic.

"You're upset and it's completely understandable, honey!

But you're taking this really hard and there are things you can do to help yourself *move on*. Get some new experiences under your belt, meet some new people. It will put the whole Raphael thing in perspective."

"Never liked that boy, anyway," muttered Dad. "Too cocky."

That did it. He had no right to say that. And, excuse me, like I didn't know Raphael was cocky. Of course he was; that was one of the things I loved about him. Raphael never seemed to have any doubts. He had confidence in his opinions, and so what if most of them involved putting other people down?

And come to think of it, what difference did it make where I spent the summer? Connecticut, Ireland, the dark side of Dingle or the rings of Saturn? I was not going to be Raphael's girlfriend in any of those places anymore.

I picked up the travel brochure, the one with the map on it. As if it mattered where a person was. I tore it into two shiny pieces. I didn't look to check, but I was really hoping that *Din* was on one side and *gle* was on the other.

"If you don't *want* me here," I snarled at my white-lipped parents, who'd probably already spent a ton of money booking me on the bike trip, "then it will be my pleasure to cross the frikkin' ocean and spend my summer *anywhere* but this frikkin' house!"

Only I didn't say frikkin'.

three

Girls with orange-streaked buzz cuts should stay the hell out of airports.

Not once, but twice, once at JFK and once at Shannon, did I get chosen for the extra special attention of a personal body search by the aromatic airport personnel. The woman at JFK smelled worse. She smelled like BO and minty gum. The one in Shannon smelled like cigarettes and supersweet floral perfume. *I guess that's why people travel,* I thought. *To enjoy the exotic smell of foreign hands, I mean lands.*

And not once, but twice, did my carry-on luggage have to endure a hand inspection. Cigarette-and-perfume woman had a fine time unloading my overstuffed backpack, unzipping my toiletry bag, complimenting me on my blue lipstick and poking around in her cheerful, nosy way through my underwear and personal hygiene products. "Yes," I wanted to yell. "I have explosive pantiliners and I'm not afraid to use them!" But why waste a temper tantrum on someone I'd never see again?

Colin, however, was another story. Him I would be seeing a lot of, though I didn't know this at the time.

When I first saw Colin I was tired and stiff from the flight, wearing my hastily repacked backpack and wheeling my suitcase behind me, hungry and wondering what to do next. I was supposed to get picked up at the "Meeting Point," but where was that? It sounded like a figure of speech, like the Point of No Return or the Last Straw or the Last Place You Look, where all lost objects eventually turn up. But the "Meeting Point": that's what it said on my now-crumpled itinerary, carefully printed out by Mom in multiple copies and tucked in my suitcase, my carry-on and the pocket of my denim jacket.

"Just in case you get separated from your things," she'd said, the big worrywart.

I pulled out the jacket-pocket copy one more time and skimmed it as I walked, wheeling my big suitcase behind me. "The Meeting Point is near the Information Desk, in the Arrivals Hall." *The Last Straw will be found at the Point of No Return. If you reach the Last Place You Look you've Gone Too Far.*

I was walking and following the signs and amusing myself by mentally riffing on this figure of speech idea and what do you know, I finally reached an open area with a big sign overhead that read, MEETING POINT. Right underneath the sign was a tall, beefy, basically okay-looking guy leaning against a column, and he was holding a much smaller, handwritten sign of his own. It read:

I come to fetch the bonnie Morgan.
Hope your arse is ready for the trip!
Your friends at The Emerald Cycle Bike Tour Company

I guess he could tell by the dumbstruck and pissed-off look on my face that it was me standing in front of him, because he unslouched himself and actually tapped his finger to his forehead in a dorky little salute.

"The bonnie Morgan, I presume!" He winked one cornflower-blue eye at me and grabbed my big suitcase before I could stop him. "I'm Colin, then! Follow me, lass."

I was about to insist on taking my own suitcase because I'd already had enough of strangers touching my stuff for one day, especially strangers who felt free to make signs about my "arse" before we'd even met. Anyway my suitcase was an expensive wheeled job my mom bought from Land's End, so it was pretty easy to manage even though it was huge and weighed a ton, and I really didn't need any help. But before I could mention any of this, Colin hoisted the suitcase up on one shoulder like it was empty.

This surprised me, and all I could think of to say was: "It has wheels."

"Does it now?" He grinned as he walked, with me half-running to keep up. "That's grand. If I had wheels, I'd skate about the whole blessed day. But I don't, do I? All I have is my merry old van. The gas-guzzling rogue! I hope it survives the trip. The bloody engine's been making a terrifying noise for a week now. Should get it fixed, eh?"

With me panting and chasing after him and him talking incessantly, without once stopping to take a breath, Colin and I hustled out of the terminal building and over to the Short-Term Car Park. His van was bright green except for the rust spots, with the astonishingly tacky Emerald Cycle Bike Tour Company logo painted on the door. The logo was, get this, a picture of a happy, winking leprechaun riding a bike and waving.

How lame is that, I thought. *My parents must have found this company on the back of a Lucky Charms box.*

I stared at the picture of the leprechaun, and the leprechaun stared back. The nightmare reality of putting my skinny arse on a bike seat for an entire week was starting to sink in, and it was not a good feeling. But anything had to be better than being stuck at home with my white-lipped, worrying parents and robot-girl Tammy, with the total lack of Raphael echoing through every square inch of my open-plan house, my no-name town, my ruined and empty life.

I'd thought about Raphael a lot on the flight. When I was feeling nervous during takeoff, I thought, *Maybe we'll crash and I'll die and he'll be sorry.* I tried to imagine him sobbing with remorse at my funeral, but I couldn't, really.

And when we were up in the sky, high above the ocean, the passengers were watching the movie and the cheerful Aer Lingus flight attendants were taking a break from their constant offers of weird snacks (Black-and-white pudding? Lemon curd muffins? Good thing they had Pringles or I would have starved.), the plane was quiet, and I closed my eyes and got sleepy. That's when I remembered some nice things about Raphael. He was a good kisser, that's for sure.

Is. Raphael *is* a good kisser. He just won't be kissing me. Ever. Again.

"Step in, then, bonnie Morgan!" Colin had tossed my suitcase in the back of the van and was already behind the wheel. "No, lass, sit up front with me! I don't want to feel like the bloody driver, then, do I? We're going to be friends in a minute and you'd be embarrassed to be all alone back there shouting up to your old pal Colin."

I climbed into the front and slammed the passenger side door. Right away I noticed the seat belt was broken. Mom had me well trained. Colin noticed me noticing.

"Should get that fixed, eh? Don't worry, lass, I've been drivin' since I was a boy-o. You mind if I smoke, Mor? We'll leave the windows open; I'm like a dog that way anyhow. I like to feel the air on my face."

Since when did anyone call me Mor? Colin was acting like we were lifelong chums, and the only words I'd spoken to him so far were, "It has wheels." Maybe that was sufficient basis for friendship in this part of the world. Maybe he was just a freak. One thing was for sure: There was no need to expend energy listening for what Colin was really thinking, because it spilled out of his mouth nonstop.

I rolled my window down halfway and looked over at him, careful not to smile. He grinned and clucked his tongue, which made the already-lit cigarette twitch in his mouth, and he revved the engine of the van. It sounded like a fleet of decrepit helicopters struggling to take off in the midst of a swarm of furious bees.

"Gotta get that fixed, eh?" And we were off.

i snuck glances of Colin driving as we made our way toward our destination—someplace north of Limerick I think. He'd told me and showed me a map but I was not interested in maps. The scenery outside was pleasant, and we were driving on the wrong side of the road, which offered a kind of thrill, but I usually find people more interesting than scenery, and okay-looking young guys more interesting than regular people. So I checked out Colin. Discreetly, of course.

Colin was not any older than twenty-two, I guessed, and athletically built, with thick, lightly freckled arms. When he moved his foot from the gas to the brake, his thigh flexed and I could see an edge of muscle moving beneath the fabric of his thin khaki pants. He was baby-faced in a way that might make you think he was pudgy, but there was not one millimeter of tummy rolling over the waistband of Colin's pants.

If a guy has a flat stomach sitting down, those are buff abs indeed.

Not that I was planning on scoring a look at Colin's abs. It just made me think of Raph again. Raphael was very proud of his abs and even kept track of his monthly crunch totals, but when he sat down there was about a half-inch of roll he could never get rid of. God help you if you noticed it too.

So Colin scored points in the bod department. Unfortunately his hair color could only be described as strawberry frikkin' blond. It looked fine on him, but still. I found it annoying.

"Are you in a band, then?"

His stream of chatter had been relentless, and I'd only half-listened since I was busy checking him out, but this seemed to require a response. "No," I said, after a moment's thought.

"All the girls I know with bald heads are in bands. What's that about, eh? If you want to be bald, be bald. No need to sing about it!" He laughed, thoroughly pleased by his own observation. "Have you got any tattoos, then?"

Well, I did not. But how would Colin ever find that out?

"Yes," I said. And then, thinking it sounded more provocative, I said, "Two."

Colin let out a low whistle. "You're a pistol, I can tell, Mor," he said. "I almost got a tattoo once, at the end of a long night of too much drink. Praise the Lord I hadna enough money on me! Me mates'd convinced me to get the 'Emerald Cycles' advert branded on me bum. What a life of regret and remorse that would been the start of, eh?"

"Don't you like leprechauns?" I asked, sounding snarky. *It has wheels. No. Yes. Two. Don't you like leprechauns?* I could still hold my end of our entire conversational history in the palm of my hand, but I suspected that this form of entertainment might soon reach an end.

"Leprechauns!" Colin snorted so hard I thought a booger would fly out of his nose. He floored the gas pedal. "Is that why you've come to Ireland, lass? To see the wee folk? Silly Mor!" Colin laughed harder and drove faster, but the laughter sounded forced. "Take it from your old pal Colin—there's no such thing as leprechauns!"

four

Why is it that anytime you do anything new that involves a group of people, the first thing that happens is "orientation"? Are human beings in such constant danger of becoming disoriented that we have to keep stopping and orienting ourselves? Up, down, inside, outside, moss growing on the shady side of trees. Like it matters.

I had crossed an ocean and I was tired and I just wanted to crash in my room and channel surf Irish TV. Instead I was squeezed onto a deep, squishy sofa between a pair of very tall blond people, listening to a sturdy freckle-faced woman spew enthusiasm.

"Welcome to orientation! The Emerald Cycle Bike Tour Company welcomes you to our fair country." The freckle-faced woman was wearing a name sticker on her right boob. It read, "Mrs. Patricia Finneran-O'Hennessey." Good thing she had big boobs.

"We hope you're all settled in and snug as bugs in your rooms by now. Isn't the inn lovely? It's lovely, isn't it? Nearly four hundred years old, can you believe it?" Mrs. Finneran-O'Hennessey-Boob clapped her doughy white fingers together politely, without making any real noise, while smiling and nodding at an elderly couple who were standing in the back of the room. The innkeepers, no doubt. They seemed about the same age as the house.

Mrs. Boob's symbolic finger clapping was joined immediately by some really loud, vigorous, whack-your-hands-together clapping. Source of sound: the two tall blond people on the sofa with me, one male and one female, though it was hard to tell which was which because they were both totally buff and sat up straight as mannequins and were wearing identical bike outfits.

Bike outfits? I thought. *Hello, this is orientation, we're in the living room of Ye Olde Quaint Charming Irish Inn, gathered quaintly around ye olde fireplace, so easy on the spandex, there.*

"*Wunderbar!*" cried the clapping girl. Her name sticker read Heidi. She was sitting pretty close to the fire, which made me wonder if spandex was flammable. Sure would be a bummer to get incinerated on the first night, especially after spending so many Euros on all that fancy bikewear.

"Take a look around the room at your fellow travelers. You'll be getting to know each other very well this week. There are no secrets on a bike tour, believe me!" Mrs. Boob laughed at her own hilarity. "Let me introduce everybody. Most of you have already met Colin—give us a wave, there, Colin!"

Colin was in the back of the room too, slouched against one of the dark paneled walls. He gave a little tip of his imaginary hat and grinned. I thought he might have winked at me too, but maybe it was just the flickering light from the fire. I made sure not to look at him again, just in case.

"Colin will drive the van that carries your luggage, and he'll take the same routes you'll be using except for the places where the roads are too narrow for the van to safely pass. He's your number-one backup plan out there. If you get a flat tire or a sore bum—it happens!—you'll be glad Colin's nearby."

Mrs. Boob took out a clipboard. What would an orientation be without sticky name tags and a clipboard, I ask you?

"Now, for the adventurers! Allow me to introduce the Billingsley family. Just raise a hand when I call your names. Edward—that's Mr. Billingsley, I see." There was a family of four on folding chairs directly behind the sofa. Apparently they were the Billingsleys. "Winifred?"

"How do you do," said Winifred Billingsley to the room. She sounded very proper and British, like Julie Andrews. She looked a bit like Julie Andrews too. I tried to picture her elegant blond hairdo after eight hours in a bike helmet, all flattened out and sweaty. Maybe she'd let me shave it off for her, heh heh.

"And we've got the two wee Billingsleys along—Derek, ah, you're not so wee. There's a strapping lad!" Derek slumped down in his chair looking ready to die. I guessed he was about twelve. "And the lovely Sophie. Do you enjoy a nice bike ride, then, Sophie, dear?"

Sophie made a pouty face. "I like my *scooter*," she whined. She was Tammy's age. Winifred shushed her promptly.

Brilliant. A week's vacation from robot girl and I get stuck with a British brat instead.

"I sympathize completely, Sophie," said Mrs. Boob, with one of those fake you-and-me-against-the-world smiles grown-ups like to give crabby children. "On my days off from work I ride a sweet little Harley-Davidson. The hog is a welcome change, to be sure."

Mrs. Boob? Biker chick? What kind of country was this? But Mrs. Boob was already on to her next victim.

"Mr. and Mrs. Faraday. Wait then, I see a cancellation marked here. It's just Mrs. Faraday, correct?"

Nobody said anything.

"Mrs. Faraday? Lucy Faraday? Are you with us?"

It took a while, but finally Mrs. Faraday raised her hand. She was in an armchair that was half-turned toward the fire. It was one of those kinds of chairs that has little wings on the side, so her face was partly hidden. "Yes. I'm here," she said.

"And where's Mr. Faraday then?" asked Mrs. Boob, in her jolly way. "Though I know how the menfolk can be! Some of 'em won't leave the office for a holiday unless it's a national emergency. He's not sick I hope?"

"Not anymore," said Mrs. Faraday, softly. "He died."

That shut Mrs. Boob up for sure. But only for a second.

"I'm terribly sorry, dear," she said, her pale face turning red behind her freckles. "I apologize for not knowing beforehand. We're so glad you're here with us during this difficult time."

I was trying not to look his way, but I couldn't help noticing that Colin lowered his head and clasped his hands in front of him as Mrs. Boob said this. Then Mrs. Boob did the same. I was afraid they were going to expect us all to pray or cry or something, but then they both snapped out of it, and Mrs. Boob was just as merry as before.

"Home stretch, now! A warm *willkommen* to Heidi and Johannes Schein."

The two spandexed blonds practically bounced up and down in their eagerness to raise their hands in the air. I clutched the sofa cushions so I wouldn't get knocked off. Mrs. Boob smiled at them. "You look far too young to be married. Are you brother and sister, then?"

"Tvins!" said Johannes and Heidi, at the same time. Gag.

"Double trouble, eh? Well I'm sure we'll all take a 'shine' to both of you, ha hah! And there ought to be another young lad here—Morgan Rawlinson?" She scanned the room look-ing for the lad she thought was me, but of course I was the only person left she hadn't called.

About this lad business—it is a fact that my parents gave me a boy's name. Fact, and yet they deny it. Whenever I complain they start chanting, "Morgan Fairchild! Morgan Fairchild!" like anybody my age has a clue who that is or gives a crap. Morgan *Freeman*, people; he's a *dude*.

So Mrs. Boob's mistake didn't surprise me. However, this was the first time someone assumed I was a boy while I had a buzz cut. Boy name, boy hair—there were definitely some chain-yanking possibilities here. But spoilsport Colin was al-ready giggling in the back of the room.

"The bonnie Morgan is a lass, Patty! That's her with the bald head up front, see?"

Mrs. Patty Boob looked at me. "Ah, I was wonderin' who you might be! Morgan it is." She looked at me kindly, like I was retarded. "Do you like Sinéad O'Connor, then?"

All bald people like each other, it's well known.

"I prefer Curly," I said. "From the Three Stooges." I have

an awesome deadpan expression when I want to use it, and I let it rip. I could see on Mrs. Boob's face she was trying to guess whether I was messing with her or not. She must've decided she didn't care, because she just went on with the orientation. Score points for Mrs. B.; it was the only dignified response.

"That's it then," she said, flipping her clipboard over. "We've two more but they won't be arriving till morning. On their honeymoon, you know! I expect they wanted some privacy tonight."

I did not need a mental image of someone else's night of passion, thank you very much.

I used to imagine what it would be like to spend the whole night with Raph, waking up together and everything. We fooled around plenty but never went all the way. Sometimes when I hadn't seen him for a few days and I'd be thinking about how great he was and all that, and I'd decide that I wanted to. But then we'd get together and I'd start to feel unsure. So we didn't. He didn't complain about it that much. I thought that meant he was a gentleman or cared about my feelings or some happy crap like that. Only after he dumped me did I realize, he probably just didn't find me that attractive.

". . . always wear your helmets . . . stay with your buddy . . . cell phones . . . maps . . . breakfast at 8 a.m. sharp . . ." Mrs. B. was orienting everyone into a frenzy, but I gave up listening. The image of Raph boffing a brainiac girl from brainiac leaders-of-tomorrow camp was now lodged firmly in my mind, and no amount of reminders to stop frequently, drink water and stretch my hamstrings was going to make it go away.

Why was I here again? To forget about Raph? No. I was here so my family could forget about *me*. This was their vacation from Miserable Morgan.

Maybe they'd enjoy my absence so much they wouldn't let me come home. My dad would cancel the return ticket without telling me and I'd be standing in the airport, stranded. I'd change my name, hitchhike across Europe, survive by eating foreign food out of foreign trash bins. . . .

"Nice to meet you Morgan!" Heidi and Johannes were standing in front of me, grinning. Apparently Mrs. Boob was done talking and we were in the "now go annoy each other" portion of orientation.

"We are called Heidi!" said Heidi.

"And we are called Johannes," said Johannes.

"I see that," I said, nodding at their name tags.

"We are taking the trip to practice English and meet youth from other countries. We are nice to meet you!" Heidi was at least five foot ten. If I stood up I'd be talking to her spandexed chest, but sitting left me in a worse position. It was hard to decide what to do.

"Happy!" said Johannes. "Happy to meet you!"

"Awesome," I said. I decided to stand. And leave. "I'm gonna go crash. Have fun."

"Crash?" asked Heidi.

I made a little sleeping pose by folding my hands and putting them next to my face.

"Ah!" said Johannes. "Have a nice crash!"

"Right," I said. I looked around the room. Mrs. Boob was speaking quietly with Lucy Faraday, and there was some hankie action going on. Mrs. Billingsley was nagging Derek to put away his Nintendo DS, and Mr. Billingsley was trying to hoist little Sophie onto his shoulder; she'd fallen fast asleep.

I thought it might be fun to say something sassy to Colin before heading back to my room, but he must have left already. I didn't see him anywhere.

five

Ireland is on Greenwich Mean time, which is five hours later than Greenwich, Connecticut, time.

Greenwich Mean Time. I liked the sound of it. There was no Greenwich Nice Time, and that was fine with me.

After the meeting I'd been so cotton-mouthed with jetlag and stupefied by all the dis-orientation that I'd gone back to my room and passed out in my stinky travel clothes on top of the bedcovers.

Almost immediately I'd started dreaming of a human-sized cuckoo clock. Heidi and Johannes were popping in and out of the little wooden doors, flapping their spandexed arms like wings. "Tvins!" they'd chirp, and disappear. "Tvins!" But then the phone rang and woke me up.

"What?" I said, groggy and cross.

"Honey!" It was my mom's voice. "How are you? Is Ireland beautiful? Are you having fun?"

"Sleeping," I mumbled. "Long day."

"How was the flight? Did you have something to eat? Did you meet the other people yet? Is everybody nice?"

"'S fine," I said. I was trying not to wake up all the way, but it was getting difficult. "'S late here. Greenwich Mean Time, remember?"

"We just wanted to make sure you'd arrived safely. Your dad's not home from work yet but he sends his love. I'll put your sister on. Be careful! Wear a helmet, okay? Love you, bye!"

"Hi!" said Tammy. "Bye!"

"Say something nice to your sister," I heard Mom say in the background.

"Something nice to your sister," said Tammy, giggling. "It's great here without you! Bye!"

Then it took me an hour to get back to sleep.

Seven a.m., Greenwich Mean time. time to rise and bloody shine, as Colin might say.

There was no shower in my bathroom, only a tub. I had to stare at the plumbing a bit for this information to sink in. *Screw it then, I'll have a bath,* I thought. I never took baths at home. Tammy still did because she was such a baby, and my mom loved to marinate in her smelly herbal bath beads from Lucky Lou's. Even my dad took an occasional hot soak when he over-did it on the golf course. In my opinion baths were too quiet. I liked the sound of shower water rushing past my ears, drowning out the things I didn't want to think about. Baths were a waste of time and hot water, a little kid thing to be outgrown.

But this bathtub was cute, I had to admit. It stood on four splayed lion feet and was much deeper than the tub at home. The water was plenty hot, and Ye Olde Quaint soap smelled like wildflowers. If I had hair I would've had to figure out how to rinse it, but that was not an obstacle at the moment.

Naturally my mom had run out and bought two of everything on the "what to bring" list in the brochure, so I had several pairs of padded bike shorts to choose from. Which pair would make my ass look less than huge? Answer: None of them, so I grabbed a pair of sweatpants and a hoodie and made it to the dining room for breakfast by, oh, 8:20 or something like that. Close enough, right?

Okay, so i was late. the rest of the gang was pretty much done eating by the time I walked in, and Colin had just distributed the official Emerald Cycle Bike Tour cell phones.

"How do I call my teacher, Miss Abbott?" demanded Sophie, randomly pressing buttons on the phone. "How do I call my best friend, Penelope? How do I call my other best friend, Ivy? How do I call Mum and Daddy? How do I call—"

"How do I call Sophie and tell her to shut up?" said Derek. "Hey, this phone is bollocks; there aren't any games on here at all."

"Children!" said Mrs. Billingsley, wincing. Mr. Billingsley snatched the two phones away from his children, causing Sophie to fume and Derek to flip open his Nintendo.

"The left button rings Patty, the right button rings me," Colin explained with infinite patience, as I slunk over to the coffee station. "Hallo there, Mor! You'll be well rested for the day, then. Quick fix yourself a plate; we'll be on the road in a few minutes."

"Not hungry," I said. I was, but being contrary had become a reflex by now. The coffee smelled awfully good. I poured myself a cup.

"Can't ride twenty miles on an empty stomach, lass. Go get yerself some bacon and eggs." Colin sounded friendly but stern. My tourmates were sitting on benches at an enormous, rustic-looking wooden table. There was one empty spot between Johannes and Derek, who was now busy "accidentally" kicking his sister. I knew that trick too.

Johannes smiled bravely at the Billingsleys, who were looking very stressed. "Brothers and sisters! Me and Heidi, we were the same," he said. "Always fighting, with the—what is this in English?" He ground his knuckle into Derek's skull.

"Ouch! A noogie!" Derek yelled.

"Ya! Remember, Heidi?" He laughed. "Always with the noogies!" Heidi laughed too. The thought of these two and their Teutonic über-noogies seemed to quiet Derek down.

I had to go past the long, tempting breakfast buffet to get from the coffee urn to the table. I picked up a plate, ignored the bacon and eggs (which looked delicious) and chose the crust end of a loaf of brown bread out of the bread basket. With my hard nub of bread and a cup of black coffee, I slid into place next to Derek.

Colin clucked disapprovingly at my meal but went on talking. "All righty, I think that covers everything. If you're done eating then head out to the front of the inn. Patty will fit you with a helmet—"

"Will we get our new bikes now?" squealed Sophie. She had tapioca smeared all over her chin, but she kept batting away her mother's attempts to clean it with a napkin.

"It's not to keep, Sophie," Mr. Billingsley said sharply. "You've your own bike at home."

"But mine is *pink*!" whined Sophie. "I *loathe* pink! Pink is for *babies*!"

I could clearly imagine myself strangling this kid, but it seemed possible her father might beat me to the punch.

"Aye, pink *is* for babies, and you're a full-grown young woman, aren't you Sophie?" Colin regarded the little monster like he was totally serious. "We haven't any pink bikes at all, never fear. And guess what?"

"What?" The girl scowled like one of those big-eyed demon-spawn kids in a horror movie.

Colin leaned in close to her. "Patty's got a skull-and-crossbones sticker on her helmet, all dripping with blood and marrow and maggots, and it glows in the dark to boot. If you fancy it, perhaps she'll get you one too." Sophie looked stunned. "That's it everyone, off you go then! The bonny Morgan and I will be out straight away."

The Billingsleys, the tvins, and the sad and subdued Lucy Faraday obediently got up from the table. I watched their padded asses waddle out of the dining room. When they were gone Colin turned to me.

"If you've got some sort of bug up your arse, tell me now, Mor, so we can get rid of it, eh?"

I slurped my coffee and looked up at him with my best wide-eyed expression. "I'm fine," I said. "Why do you say that?"

"Just a feeling. I'm good with people, in case you haven't noticed. Didn't you bring any proper bike shorts?" he asked, looking at my baggy sweatpants.

"Yes," I said.

"So how come you're not wearin' them? Your bum'll be aching six ways from Sunday in those." Without missing a beat, Colin got down on his knees in front of me. I suppose you didn't want your backside lookin' like the map of Ireland." He pulled the tops of my socks up high over my sweatpants. "But fek it, I say, because it's your arse, after all. Nobody's business but your own what it looks like. There," he said, looking at his handiwork. "Now your trousers won't get tangled up in the bike chain. That's one way to go flying over the handlebars, for sure."

Still kneeling, he looked up at me with his broad, handsome face. "How old are ya, Mor?"

"Eighteen," I lied.

"Are ya, now," he said. "I woulda guessed younger. I'm twenty meself, but only just."

"I would've guessed older," I said. "Happy birthday." He stood up, and all at once he was looming over me.

"Ta very much," he said. "Here's your phone. Right button rings me, don't forget."

After some chaos getting everyone fitted with a helmet and a bike, filling all the water bottles and going over the maps one more time, the group was ready to go. Almost.

"But *Mother*," whined Sophie. "What if I have to use the *toilet*?"

"That's why there's a diaper in your shorts, you big baby!" Derek teased, with impressive meanness.

"You can just knock on any door and ask to use the loo. People are friendly here," said Colin.

"By the side of the road's fine too," said Patty, slinging her leg over her bike. "What do you think keeps the grass in Ireland so green? Off we go, now!"

Colin was left behind to finish loading our luggage into the van. Then he'd drive along the route, doing regular sweeps for stragglers, the lost, the tired, the hopelessly sorebottomed. I didn't expect to fall into any of these categories, so I figured I wouldn't see him again till lunchtime.

Patty had explained that she'd be riding along with us today to get things underway, but for the rest of the tour we'd only see her in the evenings when we arrived at our next inn. In her state-of-the-art bike gear, Patty lost every trace of last night's Mrs. Boob frumpy look. She was full-bodied, but it was solid muscle, and those boobs in a stretch metallic athletic top made her look like fekkin' Wonder Woman.

She sailed off on her bike, gesturing at us to follow. It made me think of when I was a little kid at the zoo watching the penguins jump into the water. They look so clumsy on land, but turn sleek and graceful as soon as they dive into their native element.

I used to love watching the penguins just to see this transformation happen, over and over. I can still remember throwing a real mother of a tantrum at the zoo one time when everybody was ready to leave the penguin exhibit but me. My dad bought me a stuffed penguin from the gift shop to shut me up. It worked, but the effect was only temporary, heh heh.

As is so often the case when you're about to do something you probably shouldn't be doing at all, the buddy system was in effect. The Billingsleys had each other (poor Billingsleys; why didn't they take the brats to Euro Disney and be done with it?). Heidi and Johannes, the buff tvins, were zooming off ahead with their heads down and heinies in the air, Lance Armstrong–style.

The mysterious newlywed couple still hadn't shown up after their long exhausting night of hot honeymoon love, and that left me and my buddy, the recently widowed Lucy Faraday. Just my luck to end up riding with someone I actually had to be nice to.

One advantage of having a sad buddy was that she was quiet, at least at first. And riding a bike, which I had hardly done in years, created its own kind of conversation substitute. Without any discussion we naturally started to pedal in the same rhythm, making long S-curves back and forth so we could check out the scenery on both sides of the road.

I guess I should comment here on the Legendary Beauty of the Irish countryside. You can even get a DVD of it, if you want. There's one called *Irish Scenery* or *Irish Greenery* or some crap like that—I'd seen it for sale in the airport. Crayola-green grass, gentle low hills, winding country lanes, ancient stone walls, blah blah blah. The nearest thing I could compare it to would be my dad's favorite golf course in Danbury, only this was way better, with the occasional cow or sheep in the distance to add personality. There weren't any strip malls or superhighways or Lucky Lou's parking lots pocking up the landscape like architectural acne. Just green, rolling, timeless and mysterious beauty.

It reminded me of the way Middle Earth looked in the *Lord of the Rings* movies, which Sarah and I had been obsessed with for a while before I started going out with Raph. Raph dismissed all three films as "wildly inferior to the books." For that and other reasons, Sarah had to carry on with her Orlando Bloom fixation alone.

Here in Ireland, though, the natives were normal sized—the ones I'd met so far, anyway—and I assumed they did not have hairy hobbit feet. Though who knew, really? I'd yet to see Colin kick off his shoes.

To hook up with Colin, or not to hook up with Colin. That was the question. Actually the question was this: Why travel to foreign lands at all, if not to have impulsive, meaningless rebound flings with guys you'd never see again?

He was a trip, that Colin, but cute enough for rebound work, and he certainly looked like all his parts were in good working order. All I had to do was keep him convinced I was eighteen, in case he wasn't the type to take advantage of a sixteen-year-old girl who wasn't thinking straight due to a recently stomped-on heart. Especially a girl who'd never managed to go all the way with her one and only serious ex-boyfriend. But Colin didn't need to know that either.

"Morgan?" Who the fek was talking to me? "Can we stop for a minute?"

It was Lucy Faraday, my all-but-forgotten sad bike buddy.

"It's so beautiful," she said. Her helmet cast a shadow on her face so I couldn't really see, but it sounded like she might have been crying. "Sorry. I just need to stop."

So we stopped. I had to pee anyway.

six

Off i went to do my part for the green grass of ireland. I squatted behind a small mossy hill to be out of sight of Mrs. Faraday, and there was nobody else to watch me pee except a couple of animatronic-looking cows in the distance. Then I came back and sat on the ground next to Mrs. F. while she told me the story of her and the late Jack Faraday. There was no way out of it, but I hoped it would be quick.

"We'd planned this trip for a year," she began. Her helmet was off so I could see that, yes, she was weepy, but it wasn't like sobby, drama-queen crying, just tears going down at quiet intervals while she talked. Every now and then she wiped them away. "Jack had lung cancer. He'd done surgery, radiation, chemo—he'd bounced back from all that but we knew it wasn't a cure, just a reprieve."

"Uh huh," I said. This was definitely one of those times when it sort of didn't matter what I said, and I was glad. I just raked my fingers through the soft grass and nodded at intervals.

"His grandparents were Irish, you know," she said, stretching out her legs. Like there was any way I could have known that. "And he'd never been here. So we booked the tour, though I secretly wondered how he would manage so much bike riding! They'd taken out part of his lung."

Enormous willpower required not to make a gross-out face at that unasked-for piece of information.

"It made him so happy, looking forward to this trip. He was in such good spirits I almost forgot how sick he was." Mrs. Faraday did a brief eye wipe. "And it ran through my mind sometimes—what would we do when this was over? I think I convinced myself that he was keeping himself alive just for this. As if he really had that power."

Mrs. Faraday was probably my mom's age or just a bit older. *The Widow Faraday,* I thought, like it was a name from a fairy tale. *And they all lived happily ever—*

"Nobody wants to think about sad things," I said. Deep, huh? I knew what it was like to try to put off the inevitable. You could try and try, but it always got you in the end. "When did he die?" I hate the "passed-away" thing. People die, deal with it.

"A month ago," she said. She half-smiled. "Four-and-a-half weeks, actually. Everyone thought I was nuts to come by myself. But I had to. I'm here for both of us."

"Uh huh," I said. My mom actually pays big money for therapy, and look at me, saying all the right things for free.

"And I'm not even Irish!" She laughed. "I was born in Pennsylvania, but my grandparents are from Italy. Lucia Palombo was my maiden name."

"That's pretty," I said. Lucia was unmistakably a girl's name, which I liked. "Does anybody still call you that?"

"Only my mother," she said. "But you can if you like."

"Cool," I said. "Lucia." Score points for Lucia for talking to me like I was a real person, by the way, not some nasty punk Sinéad O'Connor wannabe, or whatever it was I looked like at the moment.

Four-and-a-half weeks. I wanted to tell her that it was only a month ago—four-and-a-half weeks, exactly, actually—that I was a long-haired, grown-strangely-quiet girl whose friends had stopped calling because of my total devotion to a boyfriend who didn't seem to like anything about me: My friends, my ass, my brain, my sense of humor, my "image," my taste in movies. . . .

I wanted to tell her, but I didn't. Too hard. Talking about your dead husband is one thing, but talking about your ex-boyfriend who dumped you—never mind, even I could tell how stupid that line of reasoning was. Maybe I just wasn't that good at talking about stuff.

"Shall we go?"

We stood up. Both of us had damp bottoms from sitting on the grass, which made me wish for a layer of padding between my sweatpants and my ass. The whole time we'd been talking not a single car had come down the road.

"Do you believe in soul mates, Morgan?" Lucia asked, as she adjusted her helmet and latched it under her chin.

I smiled, because Sarah always used to ask me questions like that. Sure, I believed in soul mates. At least I used to. Because I thought Raph and I were soul mates until it became clear that we were so totally not.

"I don't know," I said.

"You should," she said, getting back on her bike. "I found mine. And I can feel him here with me now, everywhere."

by the time we arrived at the designated ye olde Adorable Pub for lunch, I was so hungry my hands were shaking.

The full complement of Billingsleys had not made it the whole way on bikes, as darling Sophie had stopped partway and refused to ride any further. She and her mom arrived in the back of Colin's van, while the father and son Billingsleys soldiered on. The male bonding must have had a positive effect, because Derek actually seemed cheerful and was letting Sophie chase him around the yard. Heidi and Johannes were doing stretches and calisthenics under a nearby tree.

I wanted to eat, anything and lots of it, but lunch was being delayed. The Honeymoon Horrors had arrived. At the moment the new bride was pitching a fit, and Mrs. Patty Boob was trying to settle her down before leading us inside.

"I'm *quite* sure I put down that I was a vegan on my reservation form," the woman was saying. "And this is *not* a vegan restaurant. Look!" She waved the menu in Patty's face. "Fish and chips! Angus steak! 'Bangers'—I don't even know what they are but they *certainly* sound like meat!"

"Those would be the sorts of things you'd find in a pub lunch, more or less," said Patty, with infinite patience. "But I'm sure they can make you something you'll enjoy, dear. What do you eat, then? Chicken?"

The woman looked like she might explode. "I need to

speak to *my husband*. Excuse me," she snarled, with that special stuck-up attitude that comes from being able to say "my
husband" like it's some kind of prize you just won.

She was something, this pissy vegan woman. Extremely
thin, but with ample-sized and highly antigravitational knock-
ers (not a look that mother nature often creates, if you get my
silicon drift). Elaborately blown-out and tinted hair, with all
those streaks and chunks and highlights and lowlights you see
on movie star hair in *People* magazine. Ultrableached teeth.
Perfect French manicure. Teeny, tiny little Michael Jackson
nose. This chick had pimped her own ride to the max; all she
needed was a set of spinners.

All the personal maintenance made her seem older, but
she was young, maybe late twenties at the most. Young *and*
immature. This became clear when she tried to enlist *her husband* for backup against the forces of carnivoredom and he
shushed her like she was an interrupting child.

"So we'll reshoot the pilot," he was saying into his Black-
Berry. "We'll recast. I'm telling you, this show is a fabulous,
fabulous concept. Funny, contemporary, sexy. The next
Friends. The next *Will and Grace*. The next *Sex and the City*.
The next—right. Right. Right." He rolled his eyes and
looked at his wife, who was tapping her foot in impatience.

"What," he mouthed.

"I need to talk to you," she said.

He turned away. "If I'd known you were looking for
suspense—Ted, we can *add* that. We can make it so suspense-
ful you won't know what hit you."

"It's an *emergency*." Her lower lip, perfectly outlined with
lip pencil, was starting to quiver.

"Hang on, Ted," he said into the BlackBerry. "Back in a sec. What!" he snapped at his wife.

"I'm hungry," she said, pouty-faced.

"Baby, please." He covered the mouthpiece, or whatever you call the part of a BlackBerry you talk into. "You're an animal. A man's gotta rest sometime!"

"I mean *hungry*," she said. "For lunch. And all they have is *meat*."

He sighed. "Don't they have any bread?"

"I can't eat *bread*," she said, horrified. He threw up his hands and turned away from her again.

"I'm back," he said to the phone. "Okay. Okay. But I *will not rest* till this show gets picked up. You guys will thank me later, I promise. Okay. Right. *Ciao*." He hung up and turned to his wife with an expression of grave concern.

"Is it stupid to say, 'Ciao,' when I'm in Ireland?" he asked.

"No stupider than to say it in LA," she said. She sounded really unhappy.

"Come on, everyone!" said Patty, holding open the door to the pub. "Let's eat!"

Aside from getting some food into my stomach, my goal for lunch was to sit next to Colin and flirt. Lucia had gone quiet again (though now it was more of a satisfied, thoughtful kind of quiet than sad-quiet), so even though she was sticking pretty close to me, I didn't expect her to interfere.

The rest of my tour mates were another story. Heidi and Johannes's goal was to chat with me relentlessly so they could

practice their American teen idioms with a living specimen.
The Billingsleys' goal was to get their kids to eat something
without provoking any acts of domestic violence or child
abuse (I'm just guessing). And the LA couple's goal was to
suck every molecule of oxygen out of the room through the
vortex of their gigantic newlywed egos, leaving the rest of us
gasping and turning blue with admiration for their obvious
superiority. It would be a challenge to fit my flirting plan on
to the agenda of such an action-packed lunch, but I was determined to try.

"Did everyone meet Carrie and Stuart Woodward?" asked
Patty, as soon as we'd all done the musical chairs bit and
found ourselves seats around the big circular table. Colin was
on my right. (I'd practically hip-checked Heidi to make sure I
got that chair because I had a zit on my left cheek, and who
needed to see that?)

"Pippin!" said Carrie, firmly. "My name's Carrie *Pippin*.
Even though Stuart and I are married now, I'm keeping my
name, for professional reasons." She stroked her pink-and-
white nails down his cheek. It might have seemed sweet if he
hadn't been nattering into his phone and swatting her hand
away like a fly while she did it.

"What sort of work have ya had done, have ye done, do ya
do?" Colin asked Carrie, straight-faced. I almost spit out my
water but nobody else seemed to get what he'd said.

Carrie tossed her Technicolor mane of hair. "I'm an
actor," she said.

"*Really?*" said Colin, copying her tone. "I coulda sworn
you were a female." Derek giggled at this, and Colin shoved
a breadstick in the boy's mouth.

Carrie smiled, very cool. "We say 'actor' now. Only porn stars call themselves actresses. Oh, pardon me! I forgot there were children here!"

"I know what a porn star is," said Derek.

"That's enough, son," growled Mr. Billingsley.

"I do too!" Sophie chimed in. "It's when a lady takes off all her clothes and kisses and kisses and kisses! I saw it on Derek's computer!"

Mrs. Billingsley made a face and clutched her side.

"Did I miss anything?" said Stuart, hanging up his phone. "What'd I miss?"

"We were speaking about porn stars," said Heidi, with perfect enunciation. Johannes nodded and smiled, proud of their new vocabulary word.

"Porn stars! Damn, it's like I never left LA," said Stuart. Carrie laughed hysterically at her hubby's brilliant wit.

"Oh God, *so* funny, baby!" Carrie sputtered, through tears of mirth that seemed way too much for the occasion. "I keep telling him, one day they'll ask him to host the Oscars!"

What a bunch of nutcases. This was my chance to find out to what degree I already owned young Colin. I gently pressed my leg against his under the table, in a flirty "can you believe this" kind of way. He registered the pressure but he didn't look at me or say anything. He just reached over and put a piece of bread on my bread dish without asking.

Yesssss. Colin was mine.

"This afternoon we'll be riding through some truly lovely countryside," said Patty, with an air of desperation. "But Ireland is much more than beautiful scenery. This is an ancient land, filled with stories and myths from long ago. The trails we ride have been traveled for thousands of years. In fact some people even believe these roads were first laid by the fae—"

"Who requested the salad and baked potato?" Our waiter had arrived, a ruddy-faced man with snow-white hair, combed back in a neat, perfect wave.

"That would be me," said Carrie Pippin, flashing her camera-ready smile. "I'm a vegan."

"I'm from Ulster meself," he said, pouring what looked and smelled exactly like beef gravy all over her potatoes. "I brought 'em mashed; hope ye don't mind but it's the way we make 'em here." His eyebrows were as black as his hair was white. "The rest of ye are having shepherd's pie. No complaints now; it's the specialty of the house. If ye don't fancy it there's something wrong with ye and ye should see a doctor."

"May I have a look at the wine list?" asked Stuart.

"Never mind that, Pop, we'll wait to drink till we're done riding for the day," said Colin to the waiter. Then he propped his elbow on the table and gave Stuart a wink. "But you and me, we'll make up for it tonight, won't we, Stu?"

Stuart seemed completely perplexed at being shut down like this, but the waiter plopped a steaming plate of food in front of him and Patty barreled ahead with her speech.

"Now that our lunch has arrived," she said, "everybody tuck in, and Colin will tell us a bit about the Ireland of long ago."

"Aye," said Colin. "Based on how the conversation has meandered so far, I think I'll begin with the tale of Queen Maeve."

* * *

the story was a bit confusing, but Queen Maeve was like an ancient Irish porn star, is what I gleaned. She was married (to a king, duh) but she used to boast she needed thirty men a day to have sex with her, unless she was doing it with this particularly studly warrior dude named Fergus. Fergus was the only guy who could satisfy her without backup. One time Queen Maeve had to pee and Fergus held up his shield to hide her while she did it. She peed so much that three great lakes were formed.

"And to this day the lakes are called Fual Maevea," explained Colin, picking up his fork. We'd all been devouring our meals while he was spinning his yarn about horny old Maeve, so he hadn't even started eating yet.

"Fual Maevea. And what exactly does that mean?" asked Mrs. Billingsley, brightly. Moms are always looking for that educational angle, even in a story about a sex addict from 200 B.C.

"Maeve's urine," Colin said, shoving a big forkful of shepherd's pie into his mouth. "*Dead* on! This pie is bloody fantastic."

Everyone but Patty was staring at him, wide-eyed. Patty was looking down at her plate. I think she was trying not to laugh.

Even the Pippin-Woodwards were silent, except for the insistent buzz of the BlackBerry's vibrate mode. Stuart ignored it for once.

"*Fan*tastic," Colin said again, through his food. "Sophie girl, if you're not going to finish yours pass it over here, would you?"

Fek the rebound thing, I thought. *I could actually get to like this guy.*

seven

After lunch I went to the restroom (sorry, Maeve, but I'd already peed in the grass once today and we modern-day types prefer to use indoor plumbing when it's available). While I was in there I pulled the bottoms of my pant legs back down over my socks. They were still only sweatpants, but no way was I going to put the moves on Colin looking like a kid in knickers.

I rolled the waistband down a bit and stretched my arms up high in a big practice yawn, just to make sure it would flash a bit of belly button. It did. Perfect.

I didn't have any mints or a toothbrush handy but I swished my mouth out with water the best I could to alleviate my shepherd's-pie breath. That pie was awesome—I'd finished my whole plate. I'd seen Carrie Pippin gobbling down her mashed potatoes and gravy too, like a starving woman—

or, to be more accurate, like a woman who hadn't eaten any carbs or meat products in a really, really long time.

I did one last mirror check before leaving the restroom. The lack of hair and the gym-class outfit made me look unavoidably boyish, but it was the best I could manage for now. My plan was simple. Lay some big flirty move on Colin to give him something to think about this afternoon, and then, tonight, when we were all done sweating for the day, I'd take a bath and change into something frisky and get a little makeup going on to make me look older and more girl-like. Then we'd have a beer and see what happened.

This kind of man-trap thinking was both strangely enjoyable and totally out of character. I'd never been the aggressor with Raph. He'd picked me, quiet me, out of the sea of sophomore girls. I wasn't sure why, but I was so surprised and grateful that I never questioned going along with the you're-my-girlfriend-now plan he'd quickly established. Just like I'd gone along with his now-we-hang-out-with-my-friends-not-yours plan, and the Morgan-needs-a-makeover plan and all his other plans, until finally we reached the this-was-fun-but-I'm-moving-on plan.

Final mirror check. Check. Raph had made a lot of plans, true, but those plans were ancient history and an ocean away. Now I was making my own plan. And Colin was going to go along with it. I could tell.

fek that Colin.
Fek fek fek. That's all I could think.

While I was in the "loo," Euro-twit Heidi had somehow convinced Colin that the seat on her bike was loose. By the time I got outside to where the bikes were parked, he was bent over with his face next to her ass and an Allen wrench in his hand, checking the height of the seat while she moaned "Higher, Colin! Lower, Colin! Ooh, that's *wunderbar* Colin, my buttocks have never felt so good!" or something very close to that, at least in my suddenly crazed mind.

Plus—maybe this was what really ticked me off—she'd taken off her helmet and let her hair loose and it was thick and blond and falling halfway down her back, and all of sudden the tall-as-a-supermodel jock looked like the cover of *Sluts Illustrated*.

And Colin was laughing and chatting and plying his trade about six inches away from Heidi's buff, spandex-clad butt, with all that hair swinging in his face.

And then there was me. A bald under-aged shrimp in a baggy sweatsuit.

Fek that Colin. All of a sudden I felt like crap, and it was completely his fault.

I was just about to go lay down in front of the van so he could run me over by accident when he drove off (that would cost him his job, heh heh), but he spotted me.

"Hey Mor," he said, grinning. "C'mere for a minute."

Only an idiot would try the belly-button move now, so forget that. I shuffled over to where they were, trying to look as reluctant as possible. Colin handed me a camera.

"Be a luv, Mor. Heidi wants a photo taken of me and her. Can you manage it?"

"You push the little button," said Heidi, smiling.

She was pushing somebody's buttons, all right. "Sure," I said. "Smile!"

I pointed the camera at Heidi's tits and zoomed in so they filled the frame. *If only this thing had a wide-angle lens—that would be awesome.*

"Can you see Colin? And the bike?" Heidi asked, through her frozen smile. "I want to see the bike also."

"Got it," I said. And I snapped the photo.

"Danke schön!" said Heidi.

"No problemo," I said, tossing the camera back to her. My throw was wild, and she had to jump to catch it.

the sad thing about digital cameras is that you can look at the photo right away. Out of the corner of my eye I'd watched Heidi look at the camera's viewscreen and get confused. Then Colin looked too. Then they'd called Lucy Faraday over to take another picture.

I hightailed it back to my bike, tossed my helmet on the ground (it was making my head too hot, I decided) and prepared to kick off. Lucia could ride with someone else. I was in no mood to be anyone's buddy right now.

It was only after I was sitting on my bike about to make my getaway that I realized I did have a problemo, and that problemo was I needed a map for the afternoon, because how the hell did I know where we were supposed to go? And Colin had the maps. We were supposed to get one from him on our way out.

No way was I going to interrupt his worshipping-Heidi's-buttfest to ask him for a map now. I figured they must be in the van, so I hopped off my bike again and snuck over to the van as invisibly as I could. I'd grab a map and hit the road before anyone could react to my innocent, whimsical tit-photo prank.

I opened the front passenger-side door of the van and started rummaging around the mess of papers on the seat. *Map, map, where was the map. . . .*

"Hey," Colin said. He was leaning casually on the driver-side door. The window was open. "Whatcha lookin' for, Mor?"

"Map," I said. I kept rummaging.

"I've got 'em right here. No need to tear the place apart." He reached into his shirt pocket and took out a wad of folded papers. He offered one to me, leaning through the driver-side window and reaching all the way across the front seat to where I was. I took it and shoved it into the pocket of my hoodie without opening it.

"Want me to go over it with you? There are some tricky bits." I wished he would stop looking at me. It was making it hard not to look back and I was in no mood for eye contact.

"It's just a map," I said. My voice was getting stuck in my throat for some reason. "I'm not stupid. I'll figure it out."

The window opening of the van door framed Colin as if he were a photograph. "'Twasn't your idea to come to Ireland, was it?" he said. A real brainiac, that Colin. Maybe he should be a "leader of tomorrow," like Raph.

"Nope."

"Well." He leaned in through the window and lowered his voice. "Doesn't matter. You're here now. Don't act the bitch, all right, Mor? Doesn't suit you really."

I was so surprised I didn't know what to say.

"See ya later then." He opened the door and climbed behind the wheel, then reached over and slammed the passenger-side door shut, with me on the outside. "Keep your phone handy." The words were friendly enough, but his voice sounded cool. "Right button's me, don't forget."

Like I would ever, ever ask this guy for help. Jerk.

i was a half mile down the road before lucia caught up with me.

"There you are," she said, breathless, as she came up alongside me. "Sorry to take so long getting ready. I guess you got tired of waiting."

"I want to ride by myself now," I said. "Nothing personal," I added. That was nice of me to say, wasn't it? I was being considerate of her feelings, me being a nice person and all. Only a total jerk like Colin would call a nice person like me a bitch.

"O-kay," she said, after a minute. She was still riding next to me. "But they did ask us to stay in pairs. For safety."

"I'm fine," I said. I started to pedal harder. "I've got the phone. I'm totally fine."

Did I have my phone? Or had I left it on the ground with my helmet? I couldn't remember, and I didn't care.

There was a split in the road up ahead. Lucia was falling a bit behind me now. I picked up more speed.

"See you at dinner, then!" I heard her call. "Morgan, wait! The map says bear to the right!"

I barreled down the left-hand road, into parts unknown. I

put my head down and my ass in the air and pedaled as hard as I could, just like I was Lance Armstrong in the Tour de fekkin France.

"Morgan!" I heard her call. "Morrrrrrrgannnnnnn!"

And then I couldn't hear her anymore. Just the wind rushing past my ears.

here be dragons. that's what it says when you fall off the edge of a map.

But I didn't see any dragons. Just green grass and rolling hills dotted with animatronic cows. The road went up and down like dunes at the beach but overall I seemed to be climbing in altitude, and the terrain was growing more rocky and less green. There was a strange hill in the distance with a pronounced bump on top, even and symmetrical in shape, almost as if it were man-made.

My veer into unmapped territory was not premeditated, but how else was I supposed to shake my sad, nosy buddy? At least this way I'd have some privacy. When I got tired or felt like I'd gone too far, I would just head back the way I came and then follow the map till I caught up with the group.

So what if I arrived at tonight's inn after dark? This wasn't Connecticut, where no one under the age of twenty-one is allowed outdoors unsupervised and there are photos of kidnapped children on the sides of milk cartons and Amber Alerts on the news at night. This was Ireland, where you could knock on strangers' doors to use the bathroom, and you could ride your bike down the middle of the road for hours without seeing a single Lexus, Hummer or SUV.

This is Ireland, I thought as I pedaled. I'd crossed the ocean but I was still miserable and a loser. I still felt out-classed and outgunned by every random female who crossed my path, and I was still making up daydreams about happy romances with guys who clearly were *just not that into me.*

This was Ireland, and my family was glad to be rid of me and I didn't know where I was or in what direction I was heading. Worse, I had no idea where Raph was or what he was doing right this very minute. All I knew is that wherever the two of us were, I was the one thinking, missing, longing and wondering about him. No way was he thinking about me. Raph? Please. He'd have his brainiac-camp girlfriend all picked out by now.

This was Ireland, and my butt was starting to chafe and a cool wind was kicking up, and it was starting to look like it might rain. As much as I hated to admit it, I was stupid to have gone off on my own. It was time to turn back.

And I slowed and made a sharp U-turn, but I hadn't slowed enough and my bike started to skid out on the pebbled ground. I stretched one leg out for balance and the baggy fabric of my sweatpants got tangled in the chain.

And first I was flying and then I was falling, falling, falling.

i was on the ground, but i wasn't sure how long i'd been lying there. I opened my eyes.

The long gray muzzle of a horse was pushing gently against the side of my head. I felt its hot breath on my cheek.

"Fergus!" the horse cried. "Look who's come back!"

eight

Quick recap, here: there was a horse talking to me. Strange, right?

And there was a young man—named Fergus, if you can believe what the horse was saying. I had never met anyone named Fergus in my life, and now it was the second time in a day I'd heard the name. This also struck me as strange.

The man was wearing some seriously punked-out clothing—made all of leather but not the glossy black biker kind, more the I-skinned-it-myself natural look, with bits of fur still stuck to the edges. His face was in need of a shave and his hands were rough and dirty, but this was in no way dimming Fergus's grubby warrior-dude sex appeal. This guy was a hottie, even if he did look like an exhibit from the Natural History Museum.

"Morganne!" was the first thing he said to me. He knelt

beside me and cradled my throbbing head in his hands. "Morganne! You've come back!"

So he knew my name, sort of, and acted like we'd met before. There were a number of very strange events going on, no question, but at that particular moment, the thing that struck me as the strangest and most inexplicable of them all was—my hair.

My long, thick, strawberry-blond hair. It was spread out on the ground around me like silky gold ribbons. I only realized it was attached to my head when Fergus sat me up and the hair came along for the ride.

"Fek me!" I yelled. "Look at my hair!" And then I shut up, because now I *knew* I must be dreaming.

Fergus smiled, with dream dimples, no less. "Ah, Morganne. If I start looking at your hair now, where will it end? Soon I'll be looking at your eyes, and then your lips, and then all the rest of you—"

My Little Talking Pony stomped its feet with impatience. "We've no time for that now," the horse said. "Let's get her somewhere safe, and quickly."

"Samhain is right, as always." Fergus looked into my eyes with a searching, serious expression. "Thank the goddess you're back, Morganne. There's much trouble brewing. We need you now, more than ever."

Then Fergus picked me up and placed me on the horse's back like I was a toddler taking the five-dollar pony ride at Lucky Lou's. (It costs eight if you want a Polaroid at the end. Major ripoff, that.)

Some of the richer girls at school were way into the horse

thing, but personally I found horses smelly, inscrutable and unnecessarily large. I was just about to ask Fergus how he expected me to stay on board when the beast started to move, but before I could freak out Fergus was sitting on the horse too, right behind me, and Samhain took off at a trot or a canter or one of those gears that a horse shifts into when it starts to run.

There was no seat belt in this vehicle but Fergus's strong legs were wrapped around mine, and I could lean back against his chest as we bounced up and down in rhythm with the hoofbeats. My fingers were clutching the horse's wavy silver-gray mane, and my long, long hair was whipping all around me.

I like this dream, I thought. *I hope it lasts a little longer.*

"We're taking you back to Dun Meara," shouted Fergus, above all the noise and the wind. I didn't know what or where Dun Meara was—and since I'd never been there before how could I go back?—but hey, dreams aren't supposed to make sense. I was happy to play along, and what choice did I have, anyway?

Dun Meara turned out to be a small village of thatched-roof houses inside a large circular fort, ringed by a wall of mounded earth. There were people everywhere, women and men and children too, and many of them gathered to see who it was who'd come galloping up to the gate in a cloud of dust.

"Ahh, it's only Fergus!" I heard a child's voice cry. "I was hoping it would be Cúchulainn!"

Fergus slid off Samhain's back and landed lightly on his

feet. "Not Cúchulainn, child, not yet!" he said, as he lifted me to the ground. "But one who can help us in his absence."

"Morganne." It was as if the whole crowed started whispering my name, or some version of it. *"Morganne, Morganne."*

"Hey, people," I said with a wave. "'Sup?" This was like being on the red carpet at the Grammys. I'd never had such a vivid and detailed dream before. I hoped I'd remember it later when I woke up, which I was in no rush to do since I vaguely recalled leaving a bit of unpleasantness behind me. Something about Colin and Heidi and Lucia and a camera and a map—

"Have you told her of our sufferings yet?" asked a thin, pale-haired woman. She was wincing as she spoke, her hand on her belly. "Does she know about the king? Can she lift the curses upon us?" The woman looked up at me. Her face seemed familiar—she looked a bit like Julie Andrews, in fact. "Will you help us, Morganne?"

"Patience, Lachama," said Fergus, kindly. "I've told her nothing yet. She is newly arrived from the land of her own kind. First we offer our hospitality. Afterward," he said, glancing my way, "after she is fed and rested, then we may ask for her aid."

"Morganne, do you like wheat cakes?" said a young girl, tugging at the sleeves of the dress I was wearing. (All due props to the dream fashion designer for the dress, by the way. It was flowy and cream-colored and fit me perfectly.) "I made them myself and I want you to eat one because they are *so good*!"

Fergus grinned and cuffed the girl on the head. "My sister,

Erin, was a baby at the breast the last time you saw her, Morganne, and look what a mayfly she has become! Impossible to ignore."

The Billingsleys, I realized. The little girl looked like Sophie and the woman with the bellyache looked like her mother.

"*You* ignore me all the time, Fergus. But Morganne won't," Erin said, firmly taking my hand. "I will show you the finest hospitality in Dun Meara. Fergus, tend to your horse!"

Fergus grinned at me and did as he was told, and little Miss Feisty dragged me off to find the snacks.

i should have woken up by now.

That's what I kept thinking, as Erin fed me wheat cakes and honey inside the primitive but comfortable house that she'd led me to. *It's a dream,* I kept telling myself, but the food tasted so real, and my stomach was actually getting full. Most dreams—my dreams, anyway—tended to be vague and blurry around the edges, but this one had way too much information. It was jam-packed with details that didn't seem lifted out of *Lord of the Rings,* so where the fek were they coming from?

I could never make all this up, is what was starting to run through my mind. No way, not even in a dream, not even if I had Tammy's imagination (which no one does; that kid is always droning on about her imaginary friends and the strange adventures they have, and if you get sick of listening she'll just continue the conversation with her Beanie Babies).

These thoughts started to make me anxious. To calm myself, I started imagining ways for the whole experience to peter out, like a toy that needed new batteries. Maybe I'd look behind a wall and find it was a painted flat, like the ones they used in the drama club shows at school. Maybe I'd snap out of it suddenly and find myself waking up by the side of an Irish country lane after an unplanned but pleasant afternoon nap, my bike parked nearby under the watchful eye of a decorative animatronic cow.

In the meantime, though, I was there, tasting my food and feeling the warmth of a very real-looking fire, while Fergus explained about the suffering and curses the woman Lachama had been talking about.

"While Cúchulainn has been off studying the arts of war, the Good People have been at their mischief," he said. "They've pockmarked the land with their enchantments and taboos, inscribed on every pillar and stone, carved in the trees and written in the dirt. Some of our folk refuse to leave their homes for fear of stumbling over one of these inscriptions and becoming accursed, but what can we do? The cattle must be tended. Water must be fetched. Every day some new soul falls under the Good People's spells."

"Even Fergus!" Erin chirped. "He came upon one in the pasture one day, branded on the back of one of our best milch cows."

"It cast a moon-spell over my heart," said Fergus, glumly.

"Now once each month, on the night the moon is new, he is doomed to fall in love with whatever female creature he sees when the first star appears in the sky! And then fall out again when the moon is full," explained Erin.

"That sounds exhausting," I offered, trying to be sympathetic.

Fergus poked a stick into the fire. "Last month I pledged my troth to a she-goat in the hills," he said, with a bitter smile. "At least she had no father to chase me with his axe when my affection cooled after a fortnight."

"And poor Lachama!" said Erin, stamping out a stray spark. "Her taboo was carved in a stone by the Twisting Brook: 'Whosoever jumps this stream on a horse black as night will suffer indigestion at every meal for seven years' time.' How she suffers! She's grown so thin this season, always wailing and clutching her guts. If only she were astride her chestnut pony that day, instead of the black!"

"Aye," said Fergus. "And worst of all, King Conor himself." Fergus looked down, in a dark mood.

"It wasn't your fault, Fergus!" exclaimed Erin. "It happened during a hunt. Fergus shot a bird and handed it to the king, as tribute. How was he to know the bird was enchanted? It spoke its curse as it died."

"Since the king fell under the Good People's curse he cannot resist any invitation to a feast," Fergus explained. "When our enemies wish to steal our cattle or plunder our stores of grain, they need only invite the king to dinner and there he will stay, drinking and eating until morning, leaving the land undefended."

"And fouling the air with his belches and farts!" teased Erin. I could see she was trying to cheer her brother up.

"Hush, child! The kingly farts make a royal wind, and you must speak of them with respect!" He smiled and tossed the last wheat cake her way. She stuck out her tongue at him and popped the cake in her mouth.

"When Cúchulainn returns, perhaps he will know how to

make peace with the Good People." He refilled my cup with a strong, warm drink. "But we'll speak of that later, after you've rested."

Erin was entertaining herself by trying to balance on one foot, something I'd seen Tammy do many times. "Fergus, you call them the Good People yet you tell me to shun them. Why shouldn't I go when they invite me to play in the grassy meadow? Why must I always say no when they offer me their honeycombs and sweet buttered bread?"

Fergus's voice grew stern, almost angry. "Have you not heard a thing your elders have said to you? The Good People are part of the land, and we must abide with them, but their mischief knows no end, and they fill our lives with heart-break." He caught his sister by the wrist. "Take one bite of their food and we've lost you forever."

"Ouch," she said, twisting herself free.

"Who are these 'Good People'?" I asked.

My question seemed to surprise him. "It's what we call the Ancient Ones. The Lordly Ones. The people of Tír na nÓg." Fergus looked at me strangely. "The ones from your land, Morganne."

Which land did he mean? East Portwich? Old Greenchester? "You mean, from Connecticut?" I asked, dumbly.

"*Your* people," he said. "The faery folk."

It took me a while to stop laughing. Poor Fergus was confused by my reaction. "Why do you laugh when I speak of the faeries?" he asked.

"It's just, 'faery folk'—it means something different where

I come from, that's all." I had to wipe tears out of my eyes. I hate that I cry when I laugh, but I do. That was one of the reasons I stopped joking around with Raph. I got tired of him telling me my mascara was wrecked and I should go fix it.

"Oh, tell us!" demanded Erin. "How are your faery folk different from ours? Are they good or evil? Can you see them and speak to them? Do they steal away children and leave changelings in their cribs instead? Do they come out in the daytime or only at night?"

The kid wanted an answer, so I calmed myself and obliged. "Where I come from, the faery folk are this group of guys that come to your house and redecorate when you're not home," I explained. "They cut your hair and throw away all your clothes. Then they buy you new ones."

"The rogues!" said Erin, wide-eyed. "So they're evil faeries!"

"No, they mean well," I said, trying to keep a straight face. "They think they're being helpful. Sometimes they totally trash your stuff and make fun of your favorite shirt, but then sometimes they give you a plasma TV, and that chills most people out. It's all in fun."

"It's the same as here, then." Erin sighed. "Mischief is bread and mead to the faery folk."

What kind of kid uses a word like "mead"? I cracked up again.

Fergus saw me laughing and crying. "She's a queer one for sure, that Morganne," he said, elbowing Erin in the ribs.

Even in dreams little sisters eventually get put to bed, and after Erin was asleep Fergus asked me to walk through the village with him. The yummy drink he'd given me had definitely taken the edge off my worry about when and how this dream might end, so I decided to consider it a dream date and try to enjoy myself.

We stayed inside the "dun," which seemed to mean the large circular embankment that surrounded all the houses. There were goats and chickens running about, small fires burning in front of houses, women churning butter, men cleaning the horses' harnesses and people doing their end-of-day chores pretty much as they still do today, except without any labor-saving appliances or cable TV to channel surf when the work is done.

Everywhere we walked, people nodded respectfully to Fergus, and pointed and whispered when they saw me. A couple of women started to shriek and ran into their houses. Not what you'd call a big self-esteem builder. I finally asked Fergus what was going on.

He scuffed his leather-clad feet. "It's been foretold by our Druid priests that King Conor will never be cured of his curse until he is wed to a maiden of fire and gold." Fergus smiled at me, a little shy. "Perhaps they think you are the one?"

"Why me? I don't get it."

"Your hair, Morganne," said Fergus, gently lifting a wavy lock of my new Rapunzel tresses till it shone in the flickering light of a nearby fire. "Yellow and red, and it glitters like polished metal—surely it is the color of fire and gold."

"Dude, I'm sixteen," I cried. "I'm not getting married!"

He dropped my hair and looked at me kindly. "True, 'tis old to not have a husband already chosen, but you shouldn't despair of it yet, Morganne!" His eyes were a twinkling, cornflower blue. "There's many a good man who would take you to his hearth, and gladly." He glanced away again. These ancient warrior types could be bashful about girls, apparently.

"Well, I'm not marrying any farting old king, that's for sure," I said, and he laughed.

"Aye." He took my arm as we started to walk. "It's no easy task to glean the true meaning of a prophecy. Time and fate alone will reveal what's to come."

"Aye," I agreed, just for fun. Saying it made me feel like a pirate. "You're not married, are you, Fergus?" He wasn't wearing a ring, but who knew if rings were the custom here in dreamland?

Fergus's eyes turned sad as quickly as they'd grown merry. "What kind of husband could I be, with the Fairy Folk's lovesickness curse upon me?" he asked. "And when Cúchulainn returns, my first duty will be to drive his chariot, as I swore to do when we were boys together. That's no life for a woman, waiting at home and wringing her hands while her mate is off getting killed in battle."

He talked about getting killed as if it were just another one of life's unpleasant necessities, like taking the SATs. I didn't want to go there—why spoil my own dreamworld?—so we kept walking, this time away from the village and toward the field where the horses were grazing for the night.

When we got to the edge of the grass Fergus gave a soft whistle, and Samhain appeared as if out of nowhere. I petted his velvet nose as he nickered softly, in pure contented-horse language this time. Fergus took off his cloak and spread it over the damp grass. We sat down and looked up at the night sky, with Sam grazing next to us.

"See," he said, pointing upward. "The moon is waning. Tomorrow it will be gone. I'm free of my love madness now, but only till the first star appears tomorrow night."

Just my stinky luck to be having a dream date with a guy who'd be falling in love with some random livestock the next day. On the other hand, how long could this dream last? If it was a dream, that is. But if it wasn't, what the fek was going on?

Thinking about this was starting to make my head hurt. Time to change the subject.

"So tell me, Fergus," I said, pulling the edge of the cloak up around my legs. "Who's this 'Kahoolin' you keep talking about?" That's what the name sounded like to me. "And where is he, and why is everyone waiting for him to come back?"

" 'Who's Cúchulainn?' she asks!" Fergus laughed, his spirits rising again. "Am I destined to give up being a charioteer and take up the lute of a bard? Why else would you test my ability to tell you a tale you already know so well?"

"Just tell me the damn story, okay?" I snuggled into the warmth of the cloak. It was made from the tanned hide of some fairly large animal, but this was no time to get squeamish. Besides, I was finding the whole situation—me, Fergus, the moonlight—quite agreeable. Dreamy, in fact. "Pretend I've never heard it before."

Fergus smiled and his dimples started to show again. "Attend my story, then, newborn Morganne, for surely ye can have spent no more than an hour on this earth if ye've never yet heard the name of Cúchulainn!" He pulled his side of the cloak up too, and rolled himself closer to me, pitching his voice low for an audience of one.

"I speak now of Cúchulainn," Fergus began. "Greatest of the heroes of Ulster, the Guard-Dog of our people, the Hound who is fated to save and defend us all! His battle cry is fierce; his chariot makes the ground shake; when the fever of war is upon him, he can hardly tell friend from foe. An entire war band is no match for one man, if that man is Cúchulainn when he is in his fighting temper. . . ."

Kahoolin, ka-shmoolin. The night air was chilly but it was warm beneath the cloak, and Fergus's voice was a smooth low lullaby, and the story was wonderfully boring, all about war and sword-waving and thundering hooves and crap like that.

Can you fall asleep inside a dream? Apparently so, because that is exactly what I did.

nine

"Mor? Open your eyes, luv. It's your old pal Colin talking."

I wanted to stay inside the soft fur of the cloak, wrapped in the warmth of Fergus's voice, but there was something freezing cold on top of my head and I came to with a violent shiver.

"Too cold!" I said. My eyes flew open. Colin's face was very close to mine, his cornflower-blue eyes gazing at me with concern. I could smell his spicy drugstore aftershave, mixed with the faint aroma of cola and cigarettes. Quite pleasant, actually.

"You smell good," I mumbled.

His face turned pink and he jumped back about a foot. "Well, if you're busy smellin' people I guess that means you're alive," he said, with an embarrassed smile. "Can you sit up, then?"

Of course I could sit up. Why wouldn't I be able to—but

as I moved, my head throbbed and I was hit by a wave of nausea. Colin moved with me, maintaining a constant distance as if we were dancing, and I realized he was holding an ice pack on top of my head.

I looked around, turning my head as little as possible because of the ice pack and also so I wouldn't make myself puke. We were by the side of the road, in the same spot where I'd wiped out. My bike was lying on the ground, looking a bit bent, and I was sitting in the dirt in a shallow ditch alongside. The skin on my right forearm was scraped and raw, and on my right leg the sweatpants were stuck to my skin. A dark spot of blood below my knee was seeping through the fabric.

Colin was in the dirt next to me. Patty and Lucy Faraday were standing behind him, looking at me with stricken faces, like I was a heap of severed limbs they'd just discovered in a Dumpster.

"Ow," I said. This was more because of their horrified expressions than because I could feel any real pain.

"You're all right, Mor. Bump on the head and a bit o' road rash, looks like," Colin said. "The biker's badge of honor. Now you're official. You can come back and work for us next summer." He grinned and winked, but the worry didn't leave his face.

I looked past Colin and saw his van parked nearby, skewed across the entire width of the road. It made me wonder what would happen if someone needed to drive by, but two vehicles would qualify as a traffic jam around here.

"Can you tell us your name?" Patty demanded.

"Morganne. I mean, Morgan," I said.

"Wiggle fingers and toes?"

I complied.

"Brilliant," said Colin. "Now can you do the hokey pokey and turn yourself around?" Colin's deadpan was so excellent for a minute I thought he was serious.

Patty put her hands on her hips, Wonder-Woman style, and looked up the road. "You shouldn't even be on this road. It's not part of our route." She frowned. "If Mrs. Faraday here hadn't seen you turn down it, we'd have had the devil's time finding you."

It's always the way, when you get hurt: First people are happy you're alive, then they want to kill you.

"Guess I made a wrong turn," I said, trying to sound witless. People can't get mad at you if you convince them you're too dumb to get stuff right. I was still clinging to that theory, anyway.

"I'm sure 'twas my fault, Patty," Colin said, clambering to his feet. "I should've done a more thorough job explaining the day's map. If I take her to hospital now we might make it back to the inn for supper." When he got up he left the ice pack perched on my head and I had to grab it before it slid down my back.

"I'm fine!" I protested, trying not to wobble as I stood. I loathed hospitals worse than Sophie Billingsley loathed pink. Colin reached back in time to catch me before I toppled over. "I'm not going to the hospital."

"Ye surely are, Morgan," said Patty, immovable as a tree. "You've got a lump on your head like a pigeon's egg. You've got to be checked. And where's your helmet, come to think of it?"

"Must have come off when I crashed," I mumbled. "I

guess I didn't buckle it right." I made a lame effort to pretend to look for the helmet, but moving just made my head hurt, so I stopped.

"Never mind it; we've got plenty more," Patty said, more kindly. "You go see the doctor with Colin. I'm going to call your parents and tell them what's happened."

"You don't have to do that," I said, quickly. Who wanted to deal with the trans-Atlantic hysteria? Not me. "I just fell off my bike, okay? It's not an international incident or something."

"We'll talk about it when you get back from hospital," said Patty, and that was that. She put on her helmet and walked back to her bike.

Lucia was still standing there, holding her bike next to her, her lips pressed together, silently watching Colin help me to the van. She'd said nothing this whole time. Maybe she was pissed about not having the happy afternoon of Irish scenery and tearful buddy-to-buddy reminiscing she'd been expecting. Maybe she was pissed I lied about the helmet—she'd seen me riding without it. Like it mattered. It was my head, after all.

"Feel better, Morgan," she said at last, as she slowly mounted her bike. "I'll see you later."

Poor Lucia. All alone on the world's saddest vacation and she has to be buddies with the one person more miserable than her. *But those are the breaks,* I thought, as I gingerly maneuvered myself into the van. If other people had the power to make my life suck so much, it was only logical that I must be an essential part of making other people's lives suck. It was like that law of physics Raph tried to explain to me once: the Universal Theory of Sucking.

Honestly there was no reason for me to feel one bit sorry for Lucia Faraday. This was a woman who'd actually mated with her soul mate. Now he was dead, which of course bites, but how many people even get to have a soul mate? I was positive I would never find mine. I could barely get to know people before they started hating me.

Case in point: Colin. Just two days ago he was merrily chatting and teasing and telling me how we'd be friends. Now, as he turned the key in the ignition and shifted the van into gear, he looked mad enough to spit.

"Guess what I found back at the inn?" he said, abruptly. "Your helmet. Bloody stupid, Mor."

Meaning: He'd also known I was lying. So he'd covered for me, but he wasn't happy about it. He'd lied to his boss and now he had to take me to the hospital even though he probably hated me and wished I'd been found dead by the roadside, my remains already being devoured by animatronic—well, cows don't eat people, but maybe killer sheep or something. The details didn't matter. The whole situation was a perfect example of how my mere existence introduced suckiness into the lives of all who crossed my path.

No wonder Raph wanted "a change." If I were Raph, I would have dumped me too.

The most fun I've had on this whole vacation so far was when I was unconscious, I thought. No wonder that dream felt so real. I must have been in a coma or something. *This trip sucks, Colin sucks, I suck suck suck. . . .*

"What is that?" I asked, trying to break this awful mood. "That lump on top of the hill?" I pointed in the direction I'd been riding when I fell, at the strangely symmetrical bump in the not-too-distant landscape.

Colin whipped the van through a three-point turn on the narrow road so hard I thought we'd end up in the ditch again. Now the lump was behind us and I couldn't see it anymore.

"They call it a faery mound," he said, shifting into drive.

"*What?*" I couldn't believe I'd heard him right. "What's a fae—"

"Best be quiet and rest. Hospital's about twenty minutes from here," he said, cutting me off.

He sounded very annoyed.

Maybe it was because Colin said the f-word—faery, that is—but as soon as the van started bouncing along the road, I felt like I was on Samhain's back again, and the whole vivid dream or coma-induced hallucination or whatever it was about me and Fergus and Erin and the enchantments and my long storybook-princess hair came rushing back into my head.

"*I speak now of Cúchulainn. . . .*" If I listened hard I could still hear Fergus's voice. If I inhaled deeply I could smell the nearby animal presence of Samhain.

"You say something, Mor?" Colin asked.

"No." I wanted to shush him so I could hear the voice in my head better. "*Greatest of the heroes of Ulster . . .*"

"I'm itching to scold you but I won't," Colin said, after a moment. "Never mind that, I *will* scold you." Colin drummed his fingers on the wheel as he drove. "Wear your helmet, stay with your buddy, carry the phone, follow the map. What are those?"

"The safety rules," I said obediently, but I was still listening: *"The Guard-Dog of our people, the Hound who is fated to save and defend us all . . ."*

"Just a warning, then," Colin said, drowning out that hypnotic inward voice. "If you don't follow the safety rules, they'll pack you up and send you home, never fear. So if that's what you want, might as well call your ma and da and be done with it. I'll drive you to the airport tonight. No need to give yourself a concussion just because you'd rather be elsewhere."

I thought about what he was saying.

Did I want to be in Ireland? Not really. Did I want to go home? No way.

"I don't know what I want," I said.

There was a sign with a hospital symbol by the roadside, and Colin made the turn.

"Ah, who does, Mor?" he said after a bit, just like we were friends again. "But I'm glad you can tell the truth when you've a mind to. Here we are!"

this hospital was smaller than the ones I'd visited at home, and there wasn't anybody waiting to be seen but me. Otherwise the whole experience of seeing a doctor was completely familiar.

I'd been to the ER in Connecticut twice. The first time was when I was maybe four and my mother thought I was having an allergic reaction to a bee sting. I wasn't. It was just that I couldn't stop crying because I loved bees and I was upset that one had stung me because I thought they were my friends. I was goofy that way when I was little, always chatting with the bugs and flowers and stuff like Tammy still does. Anyway, Mom panicked because she thought I was hyperventilating and she rushed me to the ER. They gave me a lollipop and I think Mom ended up with some Ativan.

The other time was when I was on the freshman girls' field hockey team and I twisted my ankle during a game. The whole time I was on crutches the coach had me act as her assistant, making up the team roster and keeping score and all that. I used to like playing field hockey but being forced into a leadership position soured me on the whole game, frankly. I was no "gifted leader of tomorrow," that's for sure.

Other than prescribing more ice for my head, Bactine and Band-Aids for the scrapes and Advil for the headache, the doctor said I was fine. She made the obligatory joke about how nicely you could see the bump on my head because of my buzz cut.

She also referred to Colin as "your boyfriend" once. He pretended to be insulted because obviously he was my husband; in fact we were coming up on our twenty-fifth anniversary any day now, and it was the power of love and clean living that kept us looking so young. The doctor rolled her eyes.

"I hope you didn't come to Ireland for the crack!" she said to me. "If this is the quality of banter you have at your disposal, you must be sorely disappointed!"

Colin saw the look on my face and hooted with laughter.

"Watch your words, Doctor! She's from the States; now she thinks we're a bunch of drug addicts! Not 'crack' like in America, Mor!" He slapped his knee. "*Craic!* The pleasure of talking. The fine art of humorous conversation."

"It's the national pastime," said the doctor, as she taped some gauze over my scraped forearm. "Especially for those with not much else to do."

"Well, it's the cheapest form of entertainment, if you don't factor in the cost of your drink," said Colin. "What do you say, Doc? Will she live?"

"She'll have a bit of a stiff neck tomorrow, but it'll pass." She helped me slide off the examining table. "You might wait a day to get back on the bike. Where was it that you fell, Morgan?"

I didn't actually know, but Colin did. "It was on the old hill road," he said. The pace of his quick banter slowed, as if he were choosing his words deliberately. "The one that goes past Kelly Ryan's place."

The doctor arched an eyebrow. "The road that leads up to the mound? Now I'm not surprised at all. That's an old faery road, my dear!" she said, turning to me. "Funny things are bound to happen if you go up there alone. Didn't your 'husband' here tell you?"

"Superstitious claptrap!" fumed Colin, as we once again barreled down a narrow road in a wide van. "Can you believe such nonsense, coming from a doctor no less! An educated person, if you're convinced by all them bloody diplomas framed on the bloody wall."

"But you said yourself that it was a 'faery mound,'" I said. I didn't understand why he was so angry, but I was glad it wasn't at me for a change. "What *is* a faery mound? And what is a faery road?"

"It's a bloody mound and a bloody road that was built by the bloody faeries in the days of Long Ago!" he roared, going way too fast for my nerves. "It's a hill and a road, that's all it is and all it needs to be. Bloody embarrassing, all this living in faeryland. Makes us Irish sound like a bunch of dim bulbs. Bet you wish you were home again, eh, amongst the twenty-first century people?"

"Colin?" I felt like I'd never spoken his name aloud before. Maybe I hadn't. "What are you so pissed off about?"

He drove on for a minute, letting the van slow to a pace only a bit above the speed limit. "Here's what it is," he said, finally. "And mind you don't repeat any of this, especially to Patty. But I don't want to work for a bloody bike tour company all my life, you know? I'm saving money to go to school."

"Where?"

"DCU'd be fine with me. That's Dublin City University," he explained. "Technology, Mor. The Internet. That's the economy of the future." He tapped an unlit cigarette on the dash before sticking it in the lighter. "All over the country, the high-tech companies are starting up and the folks who get in on the ground floor are doing very well for themselves, very well indeed. It's the new Ireland."

I wasn't sure what any of this had to do with faeries, but Colin wasn't finished yet.

"Don't get me wrong. I love this bloody country, as much

as any man can love a country, and that's the truth. But it's the *new* Ireland I want to be a part of. We can't survive on tourist dollars forever." The cigarette was lit and he blew smoke out his window. "No offense to you and yours: Your dollars are much appreciated and ta very much. But why should we get stuck running the Tinker Bell exhibit whilst India and China and everywhere else gets to use their bloody brains to make a living?"

Colin's sudden intensity made him seem older, rougher, more warriorlike, perhaps—and that's when I realized: If you gave Colin a three-days growth of beard and made him live outdoors for a few years, he and Fergus would probably look a lot alike.

"But you don't believe in any of that faery stuff," I said. "So why does it bother you so much?"

He chuckled. "Because it's so hard to get away from, I suppose! My grandparents raised me on it, bless 'em. My folks'll be telling the same stories to my own kids someday." It was already dusk. Colin flicked on the headlights, which I'd been mentally willing him to do for five minutes already.

Now that I could see where we were going I stopped clutching the seat so hard. "So your parents believe in faeries too?" I asked. Crazy question. My parents believed in IRAs and good public schools and paying extra for organic chicken. Religion, hardly. Faeries? Please.

Colin blew the smoke out heavily. "They're good people, don't get me wrong. As for what they believe in—they believe you can only be what you already are, and there's no point in asking life for more. Sittin' in front of the desk at work and sittin' in front the telly at home, that's what those two believe in."

"The good people—your parents, I mean—don't they want you to go to school?"

"They think I've got a perfectly good job already." He looked at me, which I wished he wouldn't because he was driving and it did seem possible that another car might eventually come down the road at us, and there was hardly a single lane, never mind two.

"I'm on me own, is all. It's up to me, to shit or get off." He paused. "It'd be nice to have some encouragement, I suppose. But I made it this far without." Colin swerved neatly around an oncoming tractor, driving almost completely off the road to do so. "How 'bout you, Mor? Where are you going to school?"

"Connecticut." I almost blew it right then, but then I remembered, I'd told Colin I was eighteen. Now that we were pals again I wanted him to keep believing it. Just, you know, in case. "I'm starting U-Conn in the fall," I lied. "University of Connecticut. It's not far from where I live."

He whistled. "That's a relief! For a minute there I thought you'd say you were going to bloody Yale, and then I'd be embarrassed to speak to you."

I cracked up. "Yale! On my grades? No fekkin' way."

We had a good laugh together at that one, and the rest of the ride was one hundred percent *craic*. But whenever there was a lull in the conversation, I could make out the whisper of Fergus's voice, crooning stories in my ear.

ten

My parents had already called twice by the time I got to my room at Durty Nellie's, the friskily-named inn we were checked into for the night. As I predicted, Mom was in hysterical my-daughter's-dying-from-a-bee-sting mode, to the point where Dad did not even want to put her on the phone with me.

"All I want to know," he said, with excessive calmness, "is if you want to come home. Yes or no. If you do, I will book you a flight and you'll be on your way tonight."

"The doctor said I was fine," I said. "Honestly, Dad! I fell off my fekkin' bike is all."

"Morgan!" Oh crap. The language police.

"Sorry, sorry! It's just the way people talk here."

But I don't think he heard me because it sounded like there was a bit of a skirmish for the phone on that end.

"Morgan! It's Mom. I just want to know. The doctors who checked you at the hospital. Did they seem—*competent*?" She said it like it was a code word for something so dreadful it couldn't be spoken. Like: Were they dancing in circles like *witch doctors*? Did they cover your body with *leeches*?

"I'm in Ireland, Mom! It's a modern country. They have computers and everything."

"I *understand* that." She sighed, though I knew she was imagining me in the hands of a gibbering exorcist. "I'm just worried that you didn't get a *professional* exam."

"The doctor was great." I was glad Mom couldn't see me rolling my eyes. "She wore a white coat and she had a stethoscope and lots of degrees and everything. I think she even went to medical school."

"I can't tell if you're teasing me, Morgan." Mom's voice was getting shrill. "This is your *health* we're talking about. This is *serious*. This is *not a joke*."

Whenever I try to sound extra serious it just makes me crack up. "I'm not teasing you, Mom," I insisted, biting my lip. "The doctor was fine." I was starting to sputter. "She even warned me about the fae—"

But then I thought: *Shut up, Morgan*. As deliciously fun as it would be to tell my mother that the doctor believed in faeries, I didn't want to run the risk of being shipped home to Connecticut right this second. As much as I had not wanted to be here before—for tonight, at least, now that Colin and I were pals again—I was the tiniest bit interested to find out what might happen next.

"The *what*? She warned you about the *what*, Morgan?" I could imagine Mom's free hand dialing the travel agent on her cell phone while she kept me on the other line, booking me on the next flight home.

"About the f-f-f-f-f-fact that I might have a stiff neck tomorrow but it was nothing to be alarmed about. She even told me I should definitely finish the bike tour. She said it would be good for me to keep moving so my muscles don't, you know, get paralyzed or something." I said it all too fast, which made it sound fake, and of course some of it was. I crossed my fingers that the force of the nonrefundable tour deposit would help sway things in my favor.

Silence. "So. You don't want to come home?"

"No way, Mom! I'm having a great time!"

Silence.

"Don't you believe me?"

"I don't know, Morgan. It doesn't sound like you. I can't tell if you're lying or happy." She paused. "Either way, it doesn't sound like you."

"I'm happy, Mom," I said. "That's what's different." My voice dripped with conviction. "I'm having fun, that's all."

"Okay," she said. She sounded tiny on the other end of the phone. "That's great, honey. Okay. I'm putting your father on."

"Morgan! What did you say to your mother?" My dad sounded pissed. What did I do now?

"Nothing! Why?"

"I don't know, but she's crying."

Sheesh. Just because I said I was happy?

A little witty banter, a little truth-telling, a long look into Colin's cornflower-blue eyes—aside from the hallucination-inducing head injury, it'd been a pretty swell afternoon.

Even the hallucination was fun, really. I hadn't mentioned it to Colin or the ER doctor because I didn't want them to think my senses had been so messed up by the head bonk that I needed exploratory brain surgery or something. Still, the memory of Fergus, Erin, Sam and the long-ago, faery-infested place they lived remained strangely vivid in my mind. Strange too what the doctor had said about the "faery road" and the "faery mound." I wanted to know more, but Colin obviously didn't like talking about faeryland.

This was no time to lose focus, though. My put-the-moves-on-Colin plan was back in action, and I had to work fast since I'd only be here for a week. First step: This sweaty, dirty accident victim in gym clothes and Band-Aids needed to do some judicious grooming and outfit-picking for the evening, starting with soap and water.

Durty Nellie, that was me, all right. This inn had bathrooms with showers, but I needed to soak, so into the tub I went. The soap made my scrapes sting like hell but the water was warm and soothing, and I felt my stiffening neck muscles relax. I popped an extra Advil to take the edge off all my aches and pains, and by the time I got dressed I felt, not perfect, but all right.

Durty Nellie's had its own pub off the main floor of the inn. It looked pretty casual from the outside, so I put on a snug white blouse, tight jeans and little wedge heels to hoist my butt up a bit.

Even if Heidi shows up in a g-string, do not freak out, I instructed myself. *Heidi is not the person Colin told all his private*

*stuff to today. She does not get his jokes and trade witty banter
with him.*

She is merely tall and buff and supermodel-looking, with
long, blond, shampoo-commercial hair, limited English and a
gullible personality. What guy would be interested in *that*?

Shit. I was fekked. I needed to do something to bolster my
confidence, but what? Hair, not an option. Ass was already
working. All that was left was boobs and makeup. And
charm, I guess, but it was too late for drastic improvement in
that department.

Boobs and makeup it was. I put on one of my more low-
cut bras and left my shirt unbuttoned one rung below where
I'd usually button it. A little peek of lace. Nice.

Add a double coat of mascara, ruby-red lips and all the
jewelry I'd brought with me from home. Mirror check: very
nice. There was definitely a girl looking back at me. She was
an edgy, shaved-head, I'm-with-the-band type of girl, but hot
enough and totally eighteen. And she was me. For tonight,
anyway.

Colin had mentioned he wouldn't be at dinner because he had to tune up the bikes for tomorrow (he'd have
had this chore wrapped up already if he hadn't spent the afternoon taking care of me, of course). Now that I was feeling
and looking somewhat fabulous, the last thing I wanted to do
was sit around with my tour mates, fielding questions about
my death-defying bike stunt and listening to the Billingsley
children squabble.

My plan was to saunter past the buffet, grab a plate of

food and bring it back to my room, but when I got to the dining room I saw Lucy Faraday eating alone, thumbing through a newspaper and looking . . . not sad but not happy either.

Where the fek were Heidi and Johannes and the Billingsleys? The Pippin-Woodwards? Or Patty, even? I couldn't believe there was not one person available for Lucia to have dinner with. Except me.

Here I was, there she was. I could go say hello. I could find out if she wanted company or was happy with her newspaper. I could even apologize for acting like a jerk. Me apologize, imagine that.

Too hard. It was all too hard. The truth was I didn't want to sit with her, talk to her, deal with her. Not because of anything to do with her. It was because of me and what a dope I'd been earlier.

So I left (I was really hoping she hadn't seen me make the U-turn) and took my empty stomach for a walk. I'd had that big shepherd's pie lunch so I wasn't going to die of hunger anytime soon. I figured I'd get some food at the pub, later.

My walk around town was enjoyably ego-boosting, as I strutted my edgy new look around the picturesque medieval village like a rock star on a humanitarian tour. Small children stared, adults frowned or looked puzzled or made a point of ignoring me and the more punk-looking young guys smiled and called out, *Hey, hey, here's my number, call me, Sinéad, call me!* I was ready for my entrance at Durty Nellie's, feeling hungry and sassy and with a fresh coat of gloss over my lipstick.

If Raph could see me now, I thought. One of the things he used to nag me about was that I didn't "dress up" enough when we went out. I always thought I looked fine, but if I wore sneakers instead of boots or didn't put any makeup on, he typically made some kind of comment.

"I'm not here to pick up guys," I said to him once. "I'm with you."

"But I like being with someone who other guys would *want* to pick up," he explained.

"But that's gross." Why I'd bothered to disagree I don't know; it was impossible to win an argument with Raph.

"No, it's not," he'd said. "It's perfectly normal. All guys feel that way."

And who was I to say he was wrong? I didn't know anything about "all guys." I figured Raph was more of an expert on that subject than me. But maybe he was just an expert on Raph.

i was expecting the vibe at Durty Nellie's to be YBBS, otherwise known as Your Basic Bar Scene: more male than female, more under twenty-five than over, music blasting from a jukebox and everyone there to get drunk and/or hook up. (Presence of a live band made it YBBSWB: Your Basic Bar Scene with Band. These abbreviations were coined by me and Sarah. Sarah had given me a fake ID for my sixteenth birthday in the hopes that she and I would soon become experts in YBBS. We'd barely begun our research before I started going out with you-know-who.)

But Durty Nellie's was a pub, not a bar. There was drinking

and hooking-up going on for sure, but also families having supper with their kids and middle-aged ladies out whooping it up together after work. It was a real mix of people filling up the place, like a cross between a restaurant and a block party. The jukebox was a note of familiarity, but it only took Euros and was full of bands whose names I wasn't sure how to pronounce, like the Pogues.

There were round tables in the center of the dining area and wooden booths along the walls. In one booth I saw Patty with Heidi and Carrie Pippin, and a row of empty shot glasses on the table between them. Maybe it was the lighting, maybe it was the shots, but to my eye Carrie seemed to have turned a fairly vivid shade of green. Patty and Heidi were having a fine old time, if drunken chick-versus-chick arm wrestling is your idea of fun.

The bar itself was a massive dark wooden one about a mile long. One could easily imagine that it had been there unchanged for centuries, if not for the addition of that indispensable modern bar feature, the big-screen plasma TV broadcasting a sporting event. A dozen young guys were clustered in front of the on-screen game, and that was where I spotted Colin.

He saw me right away. "Hey, Mor," he yelled across the room. "Is that a faery mound on top of your head, or are ye just glad to see me?"

What a clown he was, grinning at me in the dim light of the pub with a big mug of dark beer in his hand. His accent seemed to have grown thicker now that he was partying.

"What you just said makes no sense at all, Colin," I said, ambling over to him.

"No doubt!" He laughed and looked down at the bump on top of my head, which honestly was not very big. "Ah, look at the poor little nub. It'll be prone to the sunburn, stickin' out in the open air like that. We'll have to get it a hat." His voice softened. "But the rest of ye is looking sound, very sound indeed."

Yessss.

"Thank you," I said, standing up as straight as I could manage. Good posture maximizes cleavage, as Sarah always said. I was determined to act my pretend-age and be cool and wry, with no tantrums or giggling or insecurity attacks. A beer would be a big help right now, but I wasn't going to order one myself with all these guys hanging around. That would be pathetic.

Like me, Colin had cleaned himself up nicely since this afternoon. His hair looked damp from the shower and he'd put on a clean blue oxford shirt. It made the blue of his eyes practically glow, like the eyes of a Siamese cat.

"What'll ye be drinking, Mor?" he asked, right on cue. "You can have anything you like as long as it's beer. We have laws about such things in Ireland."

"What's that?" I asked, nodding at his drink.

"That's Guinness, love. It'll make a man out of ye, though that would be a bloody shame, wouldn't it?" I think he might have stolen a look at my chest, but if he did it was quick. "Taste and see what you think."

He held the giant mug to my lips, and I slurped. It was beer all right, but dark brown and bitter, nothing at all like the Coors from a keg and rum-and-Cokes everyone served at parties at home. I didn't hate it, exactly, but it would take some getting used to.

He saw the look on my face. "Too much too soon, eh? We'll start you off gently then. Pat! Beamish for the young lady, please!" Before I could even ask what a Beamish was, Colin had slapped money on the bar.

"Put your wallet away, Colin, this one's on me!" Stuart Woodward emerged from the pack of men hooting and cheering in front of the TV. An American Express card dangled from his fingers; it was one of those fancy plutonium ones that my dad refused to get because the annual fees were so expensive. (Dad was a great one for tearing the junk mail into confetti before throwing it in the trash; it's his form of stress relief: "Do they think"—*rip*—"I am made"—*rip rip*—"out of *money?*" *rip rip rip*.)

"I'm buying for Morgan here, but you can get my next one if you like," said Colin agreeably. Stuart was looking bleary and happy, and he draped his arm around Colin's shoulders like they were brothers.

"Will do, man! You call me when you're dry!" He waggled his hand in a little "call me" gesture next to his ear and cracked himself up. Then, still chuckling, he wandered back in front of the television, where I saw him high-five some bewildered, beer-wielding men. Luckily the men were much more interested in the game than in Stuart's goofball behavior, and they tolerated the drunken foreigner without one person threatening to clock him in the face. A friendly country indeed.

I turned back to the bar in time to see a tall mug of pure foam being placed in front of me.

"Thanks, Pat!" said Colin. "You've outdone yourself."

Pat looked at me with the narrowed eyes of a suspicious barkeep. In Ireland the drinking age is eighteen (I'd checked, believe me), so I wasn't too worried, since I'd been passing for twenty-one back at home. But I'd left my fake ID in my room. It would be a drag, not to mention way uncool in front of Colin, to have to go get it.

I widened my eyes and prepared to exude eighteen-year-old flakiness. Luckily Pat was in a forgiving mood. "That's not chocolate milk, there, young lady," was all he said. "I hope ye've had something to eat."

"She'll be sharing my bangers and mash; thanks for the grandmotherly concern, Pat." Colin picked up a fork from the bar and gestured with it. "Ye can bring our food any time this year or next, by the by—no rush, mate!" Pat rolled his eyes but the mob at the far end of the bar was clamoring for his attention, so he left us.

"It's twenty minutes already," said Colin, not sounding perturbed at all. "How long does it take to grill some bloody bangers?"

"What's 'bangers'?" I said.

"Ye'll see. Try the Beamish first, though, while your taste buds are still pristine." Before my eyes, the mug of foam was gradually transforming itself into a creamy, cocoa-brown liquid.

"Is it beer?" I asked, lifting the heavy glass to my lips.

"It's stout, Mor," Colin said, with reverence. "Drink of the gods."

I was planning an experimental sip, but the Beamish was so good I took a nice long chug instead. Smooth, not as bitter as the Guinness, toasty and almost sweet and practically chocolatey, like the bartender had said. Yum. I took another drink.

As I did, the bartender slid a plate of what looked like fat, grilled human fingers in front of Colin.

Colin clapped me on the back. "Good girl! That Beamish'll put hair on your chest, if not your head. Now munch on some bangers; it'll build your strength."

I stared at the plate of greasy digits in front of me. They were truly horrifying. It looked like you might find a wedding ring on one of them. Or a fingernail.

"Relax, luv! It's just sausage and mashed potatoes." Colin stabbed one with his fork and took a hearty bite.

I used my fork to coax some mashed potatoes out from underneath the sausages, but they were all covered with banger grease. I concentrated on the Beamish instead. It tasted so rich it was more like food than a drink, anyway.

"Bloody fantastic game!" Stuart shouted. He seemed to have acquired an accent in the minutes since we'd seen him last: a little Irish, a little Beatles, a little Monty Python. "It's brutal!"

"It's rugby, mate," Colin agreed. "Not some pussy game like your American 'football.'"

"Eeee-*lectrifying*. I love it!" Stuart leaned against the bar for support.

Patty and Heidi strode up to the bar. Heidi was nearly a foot taller than Patty and agewise they were probably fifteen years apart, but the evening's revelries seemed to have forged some deep bond of sisterhood between them. The other thing between them was Carrie Pippin, looking greenish and very loose. Her arms waved about randomly, like she was treading water.

"Do they use animal products at any point in the brewing process?" she was asking, with difficulty.

"It's whiskey, lady! Not beef gravy!" Patty signaled the bartender with three fingers in the air. He seemed to know just what she meant.

"Yes, but sometimes it's hidden—there's rennet in cheese and horse hooves in Jell-O. Not everybody knows that. I know that, but not everybody does. Well, *you* do, because I just told you—"

"Here's some Jell-O for ye," said Pat, amiably, as he poured three shots. "They call this flavor Black Bush."

"Like black cherry?" Carrie giggled. "That was my favoritest, favorite Jell-O flavor, when I was little—"

"Drink!" ordered Heidi. *"Eins! Zwei! Drei!"*

And Patty, Heidi and Carrie threw back three simultaneous shots.

"She'll be flying high in a minute," said Colin, elbowing me and looking over at Carrie. "P'raps she and Stewie-boy here will forget they know each other. They can meet and fall in love all over again, even better than before. Eat up, Mor. The rest is yours."

He pushed the dish of food in front of me, but I was more interested in the fresh mug of Beamish Pat provided, as Stuart signed off on a new round of drinks for the three of us.

"Tell me more about rugby," Stuart slurred to Colin. I tried nibbling the end of one of the bangers. It wasn't horrible, just a strong pork sausage taste and kind of chewy. They were cold now, which didn't help. I washed the taste out of my mouth with more Beamish.

"Rugby!" answered Colin, pounding the bar with delight. "The ultimate sport. A little rough sometimes. When the boys are in a fightin' mood the game gets bloody as Cúchu-lainn's wedding."

"Kahoolin? What team does he play for?" said Stuart, giv-ing me a wink.

Cúchulainn? I could have sworn that's what he said, but wasn't that the name from my crazy dream? My head-bonked hallucination?

I speak now of Cúchulainn, greatest of the heroes of Ulster.... There was Fergus's voice, whispering in my ear like he was some guy in the bar.

Maybe it was the beer, stout, whatever, but the room was starting to spin. I grabbed Colin's arm.

"How did you know about Cúchulainn?" I said.

"It's bloody Ireland, Mor; everybody knows about Cúchulainn!" He looked at me like I was unhinged. "He's like—who's that bloke you have in America? Davy Crocker!"

"Betty Crocker!" Stuart was getting sloppy. He'd already offered to get Pat bit parts in movies. Pat, admirably, de-clined, claiming he was only interested in playing romantic leads or action heroes or, preferably, both.

"You mean Crockett. Davy Crockett," I said, impatiently. "What does this have to do with—"

"Crockett, right," said Colin, keeping one eye on the TV. "Is he the one with the apples?"

"No, she wrote cookbooks!" crowed Stuart, helpfully.

"No!" I said, trying to turn my back to Stuart. "That's Johnny Appleseed. But what about Cúch—"

"My *point* is," Colin said, cutting me off, "in Ireland, Cúchulainn is like Davy Crocker or Johnny Appleseed. Part of the national bullshit, you know." He started to laugh. "Except your Johnny skipped about the flowery fields scattering bits of fruit across the land, but Cúchulainn—he bloody chopped off heads and whacked off limbs till the ground was soaked with gore and guts and—GO! Go go go go!"

All the guys in the bar started screaming at the television.

"Fekkin' brilliant!" moaned Stuart in ecstasy, when the play was done. "Has anyone ever done a rugby movie, I wonder?"

My head was pounding from all the screaming.

"Well sure, there's that one about the cannibals," said Colin.

"Did I say cannibals?" Stuart giggled. "Damn, I must be drunk! No, I mean a *rugby* movie. Has anyone ever done a *rugby* movie—"

"It's cannibals *and* rugby," explained Colin, not entirely sober himself. "See, a whole rugby team goes down in a plane crash in the high snowy mountains. And half of them get killed in the crash but the other half live."

I wasn't listening. I knew—*I knew*—I had never heard of Cúchulainn before. Before my head bonk on the faery road, that is.

So—my dream, hallucination, *whatever*—what *was* that?

His battle cry is fierce; his chariot makes the ground shake. . . .

"Dude, I thought you said it was about cannibals?"

"It's rugby *and* cannibals, that's what I'm telling ye! The survivors were trapped in the snowy wilderness for months. They had to eat bits and pieces of their dead mates until they got rescued."

Something was strange, very strange indeed.

. . . bits and pieces of their dead mates . . .

"Raw or cooked?"

"Raw, I'm certain of it. How could they bloody cook anything in the snowy wilderness? It's not like they had a microwave."

I was staring at the bangers. The bangers were staring back at me. I was starting to not feel so well.

. . . he chopped off heads and whacked off limbs till the ground was soaked with gore and guts . . .

The conversation around me started to recede, as a kind of rushing noise filled my ears, almost drowning out Stuart's voice.

"Rugby! Plane crash! Cannibals! Now *that* would make an incredible film!

"It already *did*, mate. That's what I'm telling ye! And you know what else? It's a bloody true story!"

"GO!"

The room went wild. Even Patty and Heidi and a redfaced Carrie were screaming at the TV now.

"GO! Go go go go go go!"

That's when I raced off to the bathroom to puke.

eleven

"*go! go go go go go!*"

I drained the mead with a slurp. A deafening cheer shook the air around me.

"Drink hearty, Morganne! We drink to your health and the health of the king!

Double dose of Advil plus empty stomach plus two pints of stout and a head injury equals—

Me, puking and passing out on the bathroom floor of a bar, excuse me, pub, an ocean away from home?

Nope. It equals me, with long wavy locks of reddish-gold hair tumbling down my back, in a flowy cream-colored dress straight out of the Disney Princess fashion show. I was standing on a great wooden table with one foot on top of a barrel and what looked like two hundred extras from *Braveheart* egging me on as I chugged a goblet of mead.

I don't even know how I knew it was mead, but I did.

Sweet, honey-flavored wine. It was a forty-ounce goblet at least, but I showed no signs of queasiness. In fact I felt quite confident that I could drink anyone in the room under the table and beat them in a footrace too.

I wiped my lips and looked around at my adoring fans. Fergus was at my feet, a cute little mead-mustache on his upper lip.

This was not a dream. Oh *fek*.

"Fergus," I said, scrambling down off the table and into his arms. "We need to talk. *Now*."

On the way out of the crowded banquet hall i'd been invited to compete in several wrestling matches and an archery contest, but I managed to evade all my challengers and sneak out through the scullery door with Fergus. The noise of the feast carried through the night air, rising and falling but never stopping, like the roar of the surf.

We were at the castle. King Conor's castle, to be precise. It had been two days since Fergus had woken up in the grazing meadow alone, the animal skin still warm from where I'd fallen asleep next to him.

"But it was only this afternoon I had the bike accident!" I shrieked. Okay, I confess. I was freaking out. Who wouldn't? Beamish turning into mead, days randomly inserted in the calendar, unplanned outfit changes, hair going from short to long like one of those Rapunzel Barbies Tammy loved to play with, the kind where you spin the little plastic arm around and the hair gets longer and longer—

"Morganne!" Fergus said, sharply, interrupting my freak

out. "This Barbie you speak of sounds like a terrible sorceress indeed! But you are safe now, in King Conor's realm. No harm will come to you, I swear it."

Fergus is real, I thought. He's a long-ago warrior-dude and somehow I have slipped into his world, myself and yet not-quite myself. Myself, with a different 'do and a bit more sporty and able to hold my liquor better.

"I swear it, on my sword and my honor," he said again, firmly taking me by the shoulders. I looked up at his handsome, young-yet-weathered face, his striking blue eyes. Possibly the most trustworthy sight I'd ever seen.

"I'd better tell you who I really am," I said.

by the time we'd found a quiet place to sit, near the royal barn, I had explained to Fergus who I was. Or who I thought I was. Or who I used to be. Or who I would be, someday. It was all pretty confusing to me, but he didn't seem terribly surprised.

"It's just as it was foretold in the Druid's prophecies," he said. "That ye'd come and go, and your time with us would be as fleeting in your mind as the petals of a cut rose. That we would hold your memories for ye, as a mother remembers her infant's face at the breast forevermore, though the child grows and forgets. That ye'd walk among us brief as the sunrise, but the shadow of your presence would remain—"

"I get it," I said. It was rude to interrupt, but these prophecies got annoying fast. "So where am I? Is this the past? Is it a myth?" I looked around at the starlit meadows, the low wooden fences, the stone walls and grazing animals.

Beautiful long-ago Ireland, a page from Mother Goose—who could tell them apart? "At first I thought it was a dream—"

Fergus sighed. "Perhaps it is a dream, but of your brain's making or mine or some other creature's altogether we can never be sure. Where did you say you'd come from, Morganne?"

"Right before this I was in Durty Nellie's." I was chewing my nails, but then I stopped because it didn't seem like something the long-haired Morganne version of me would do. "We were watching rugby on television and I'd had too much to drink."

"The last part I understand," he said, nodding. "Too much mead can weaken the arm of the finest swordsman."

"I guess," I said. "Before that I was in Connecticut. It's—very far from here. Across the ocean."

Fergus looked at me like I'd just started to smell bad. "You've come from England, then?" His hand went to the hilt of his sword.

"No, I mean across the *ocean*," I said quickly. "It's in the other direction."

His sword hand relaxed. "You mean the Great Water! But that's the end of the world!"

I shook my head. "Actually there's a continent on the other side. Nobody here knows about it yet except for some Vikings, I think. Or wait—maybe the Viking thing hasn't happened yet. Sorry, I'm just not a hundred percent sure when we are, right now." This was the first time in my whole life I'd needed any knowledge of geography or history outside of a test. Clearly my grasp of both subjects was pathetic.

"Interesting," Fergus said, with growing intensity. "So there's land on the other side of the Great Water. Is it fertile land? How many days is it, do you think, by boat?"

Me and my big mouth. Raph, in case I haven't mentioned it before, was a major *Star Trek* fan. It was part of his geeky genius-boy persona; and when the show came out on DVD, he'd made me watch all three seasons. It was incredibly goofy, but after a few episodes you start to get into it.

Anyway, at that moment I could clearly imagine Fergus building a huge raft with some crazy peat-powered engine and discovering North America a thousand years too soon. That would be bad. Whenever the *Star Trek* dudes messed up some other planet's history, it was always really bad news.

"Not days, Fergus. Months. But forget it, please, okay?" I said nervously. "Because I think I just violated the Prime Directive or something. Don't ask me what that is—just, trust me. You have to forget what I said. Promise?"

He pushed a curling tendril of my hair behind my right ear and let his fingertips linger on my face. "If you command it, I've already forgotten," he said. "And so have you, it seems. You don't remember ever being here, do ye, before Samhain and I found you by the road? You don't remember us at all?" He looked at me searchingly, in a way that made me wonder just how much I wasn't remembering.

"Sorry," I said, gently. "I wish I did."

"Aye. It's as it was foretold." Fergus shook his head. "We're all victims of enchantments, in one way or the other." He looked down, embarrassed. "This month I've fallen in love with a toad. Can ye believe it?"

I couldn't help laughing. "It's okay, Fergus. In my world,

there's a saying: You have to kiss a lot of frogs before you find your prince. Or princess. Whatever."

Fergus got a dreamy look in his eye. "If I could catch her I'd kiss her, for sure! The web-toed vixen lives on a lily pad in the center of the swamp, just out of reach. You should see her, Morganne! The color of earth she is, with two soulful eyes sticking up wartlike on the sides of her head, gazing at ye like they're telling ye all the secrets of the world. . . ."

The poor guy. But love is blind, as my mother used to say much too often after I started dating Raph. "She sounds lovely," I said. "How did you two meet?"

Fergus sighed. "On the night of the new moon, I secluded myself amongst the creatures of the swamp until the love spell took hold of me again."

"Why the swamp?" I asked.

He gazed up at the moon that now ruled his heart. "Better I spend a fortnight pining over a salamander than break the heart of another innocent lass with my mindless, enchanted wooing."

"That's very considerate of you," I said, impressed. I couldn't imagine Raph being that concerned about a girl's feelings.

Fergus took my hand and held it firmly. "The spells must be broken, Morganne. And soon. Everyone believes that's why you've come back. It's been foretold—"

"—that I'm the one to fix everything! I know, I know. I'd help if I could, Fergus," I said. "But I don't know what to do. Honest."

"Fergus! Morganne!" Erin came running out of the darkness, shouting for us. "Where are you? Fergus!"

Fergus was up in a flash, his weapon half-drawn and a fearsome warrior-dude look on his face. If there were limbs to be lopped, this was your man.

"I'm here!" he barked. "What is it? Has the king's stronghold been attacked?"

Erin was panting. She shook her head.

"No." She gasped. She pointed at me. "Her! They want— Morganne—"

"Who wants her?" I could swear Fergus got taller all of a sudden. "They shall soon know the feel of my blade, whoever they may be!"

And here they came, straight out of an angry mob casting call, carrying torches and everything. It was the same supportive crowd who'd just been singing my praises inside the castle. I'd read *US Weekly* enough to know the public was fickle, but this was ridiculous.

"With all due respect!" shouted a white-haired man who seemed to be leading the charge. "'Tis the wedding night of Morganne, and we'd be grateful if ye'd come with us immediately."

The woman with the bellyache was right next to him, carrying a torch and rubbing her side. "The sooner the better," she moaned. The crowd roared in agreement.

Fergus had started to froth at the mouth and he looked like he might start lopping any second now, so I stepped in front of him, my restraining hand on his sword arm.

"Everybody relax!" I said. "When it's my wedding I promise you'll all be invited. But today's not it, okay? So chill."

"You must marry the king, Morganne! It's our only hope," said the man. The crowd murmured in support. "Ye've heard the prophecy!" the man continued, his dark eyebrows wiggling with emotion. "We've all seen you now, and we all agree. The maiden of fire and gold—it's you. It has to be."

I put my hands on my hips, Wonder-Woman style. "Is that what this is about?" I knew there was a reason I'd always hated strawberry-blond hair. "Listen, in my real life I don't even *have* hair at the moment. So this chick in the prophecy? It's not me, guys." I looked out over the mob, but no one seemed persuaded. "Not to mention I'm still kind of on the rebound from my last boyfriend," I added. "Your king deserves better."

"Prove it! Prove you're not the maiden of the prophecy!" yelled someone from the crowd. "Or we shall take you to the king by force!"

They looked like they meant it too. I glanced behind me at Fergus, who would clearly go down fighting if I let him, but he was outnumbered by, oh, two hundred to one. Better to keep negotiating. "That's not very romantic," I said, stalling for time. "Doesn't the king have anything to say about this?"

The man sighed. "The king is accursed! He cannot leave the feast till sunrise, and he'll be eating and drinking the whole night long. We fear he will eat till he bursts."

"Well, you should have thought of that before you threw a party," I quipped.

Clearly it was the wrong thing to say. "The king could die! Take her now! Quickly! Let the Druid priests wed them at once!" Before you could sing, "Here Comes the Bride," four guys had grabbed hold of me and eight more—with extreme difficulty—had pinned Fergus to the ground. Erin started screaming and pointing again but nobody paid any attention.

As they carried me through the streets back to the feasting hall, where my royal husband-to-be was helplessly gorging himself in preparation for our union, all I could think of was how my parents had been worried I'd come home from Ireland with a tattoo or a pierced tongue or something. Imagine the looks on their faces when they found out I'd gotten married. To a king with an eating disorder, no less.

Tammy would be furious. It was her lifelong dream to be a flower girl at somebody's wedding, and she didn't care whose. Unfortunately we had no relatives of marrying age at the moment. All the cousins were either much older and already married or younger than me.

How silly to be thinking of my family now. My parents weren't even born yet and neither was Tammy. And here I was, being passed over the top of the mob like I was crowd surfing in a mosh pit. I was never the type of girl to dream about storybook weddings, but honestly. A veil? Flowers? How about meeting the groom beforehand? Anything would have been better than this.

I heard a sound like the roaring of a bull, and it seemed to be getting closer. Fergus to the rescue, perhaps? I hoped that's what it was. It was a thundering, rushing, screaming sound, and it kept getting louder.

Erin pointed and screamed, until finally her piercing little-girl's voice cut through the din.

"It's Cúchulainn!" Erin cried. "He's come back!"

twelve

Red carpet at the Grammys does not begin to approximate the star-struck madness, the fan-boy hysteria, the photo-op-ready theatrics (even though cameras were a long way from being invented) that surrounded Cúchulainn's arrival at the dun.

First, the limo, I mean chariot, which was being pulled by two enormous and heavily muscled horses. One black, one white. Both of them were breathing fire. I'm not kidding.

Next, the swans. A dozen of them, tethered to the chariot and flying and squawking overhead in great klieg-light-style circles. The noise was tremendous, as were the droppings.

Second to last, the heads. The severed human heads. There were seven of them, tied to the sides of the chariot and bouncing along like so many fuzzy dice dangling from the rearview mirror of my dad's Subaru.

And last but not least, the man himself. Cúchulainn. Not

entirely what you'd expect from the rock-star buildup, frankly. Medium-sized, dark-haired, and kind of a skinny guy. More chess-team champion than football-hero material.

But that's before you factor in all the Industrial Light and Magic. This guy was oozing special effects. A funnel of smoke was rising from the top of his head like a tornado. Flashes of light seemed to shoot out from his forehead every time he turned his head. His eyes were glowing fiery red; overall I'd say he seemed pretty worked up.

"You!" he bellowed. "With the hair!"

The crowd fell silent. They put me down and stood there shuffling their feet, like they got caught stealing a cookie.

"Good timing," I said, smoothing my rumpled dress. "You must be Cúchulainn, right? I've heard a lot about you."

"Morganne. The news of your return fills the people with—excitement." He looked at the mob sternly, and they hung their heads.

"Yup, Morganne, that's me," I said, though I still wasn't entirely sure that it was.

"Then I ask you, Morganne, to tell us true." His voice rose, loud enough to carry over the assembled crowd. "Are you willing to wed the king?"

I didn't want to offend anybody. This group was high-strung, and they were still carrying torches. "It's a tough question," I said, diplomatically. "He's a great king and all. But truthfully—no." Some people murmured unhappily at this. "I'm just not ready for that type of relationship," I explained. The rumblings of the crowd got louder, angrier.

Cúchulainn raised his fists in the air and bellowed. "Then the maiden of fire and gold is not she!"

The crowd went nuts.

"*Her*," I was thinking. Shouldn't that be, "The maiden of fire and gold is not *her*"? But maybe grammar hadn't been invented yet. Come to think if it, we probably weren't really speaking English either. A person could get a headache trying to figure this out.

"Listen!" Cúchulainn silenced the crowd with a hand. "I have slain the seven troll-like brothers of the great witch of the hills! And a foul-smelling lot they were! And why did I slay them, you ask?"

Did this guy need a reason to lop off heads? I doubted it, but the rhetorical question sure helped him work the crowd.

"Why, Cúchulainn? Why?" The mob was hanging on his every word. Cúchulainn smiled a grim, heroic smile. The tornado coming out of his head whirled more violently.

"I slew them so that the witch would be forced to tell me the way to remove the enchantments that plague our king and our people!"

The crowd went nuts again, like there was a blinking applause sign somewhere reading, GO NUTS.

"Hear me!" roared Cúchulainn. "These are the witch's words, exactly as she spoke them to me:

" 'What's lost in the earth must be found,
" 'But the earth must be turned without tilling.

" 'Wed fire and gold to the king,
" 'But the lady herself must be willing.

" 'Let rivals come forth to do battle,
" 'But the war must be won without killing.' "

"Only when these three conditions are fulfilled will the curses be lifted from our people and the spells erased from our land, our trees, our stones and our livestock." Cúchulainn's eyes were glowing red again, which would be awesome if you were playing laser tag, it occurred to me. "The king will be made well and all will be as it was. And never again will the faery folk afflict us with their curses of mischief!"

"Woot!" I yelled, expecting the crowd to go nuts along with me. But they just stared.

"Woot," I repeated, awkwardly. "It means, you know, 'Yay!' " No response. My bodyguards gripped me even tighter.

"Aaaaaaaaaarggh!" I knew that bellow right away. Fergus had finally managed to escape, and now he had caught up with us. His clothes were torn and there was blood on his chin. I have to say, the look suited him.

"You heard the witch's prophecy," shouted Fergus, fighting his way to the front of the mob. "The maiden is not willing. She is not the one foretold to wed the king. Now leave her be."

Reluctantly my captors let me go, and the mob started to break up. Fergus was next to me in a flash.

"Are you all right?" he said.

"I'm fine," I said. "But I don't understand the witch's prophecies at all."

It wasn't till he saw Fergus that the horror-movie glow in Cúchulainn's eyes faded and the tornado above his head evaporated in a wisp of smoke.

"Fergus! My brother!" Cúchulainn cried, leaping out of his chariot. "Awesome to see you, dude!"

"Dude!" said Fergus, clapping Cúchulainn on the back. "Welcome home."

the "awesome, dude" thing bothered me, and here's why.

It reminded me of how Raph talked with his friends.

So much so that, as Fergus and Cúchulainn sat together in front of the peat fire they'd built after the mob had scattered, trading tales of their adventures in the months since they'd seen each other last, I could close my eyes and imagine Colin and Raph hanging out together talking guy talk, even though the two of them had never met and, obviously, never would.

But Fergus did have this rough-hewn, red-headed resemblance to Colin. And Cúchulainn reminded me of Raph in other ways—like how he was so BMOC, always grabbing the spotlight, automatically taking charge and expecting everyone to do as he said. Physically, though, Cúchulainn looked more like a younger version of Stuart Woodward than Raph. Dark-haired and wiry, only medium tall but acting taller. Similar personalities, though.

Ewwww, I thought. At the rate he's going Raph could grow up to be a self-centered, BlackBerry-wielding fool, just like Stuart. *Double ewwww.* That would not be very awesome, dude, at all.

If Raph were really here, of course, he would look at the awesome-dude phenomenon in a more *Star Trek*–type way, in which case it made sense (to the extent that any of this made sense), because whatever ancient Celtic language we were actually speaking was obviously being filtered through the universal translator of my own twenty-first-century Connecticut high-school-student brain.

I hoped that was the explanation. It was one thing to be stuck here as Morganne, not knowing if or when I'd turn into myself again. But if all my worlds were somehow colliding and combining—Ireland, Connecticut, Ancient Long-ago Wheneverville—it made me nervous, is all. I wasn't sure which reality was the realest one. Or which one I wanted to be realest.

What if I never get back? What if I never see my family again? What if I stay Morganne forever, and these people are my family now?

Erin was playing with my hair, and we stayed quiet by the fire as the guys yakked into the night. Even Erin was about the same age as robot girl. Hyper and fidgety like Tammy too.

"Morganne, what do *you* make of the witch's riddles?" asked Fergus.

I didn't realize till he spoke to me how close I'd been to dozing off by the fire.

"Since I'm not destined to marry the king, we should try to figure out who is," I said, drowsily. "How do people hook up around here?"

"When we attack a neighboring kingdom, we'll often steal their women," explained Cúchulainn.

"That seems a little harsh." I yawned. "Maybe we should write a personal ad or something. What was the first riddle again?"

"'What's lost in the earth must be found,'" recited Fergus. "But what has been lost? 'Tis a riddle indeed."

"It's the last one that troubles me most," grumbled Cúchulainn. "How can a war be won without killing?"

Erin had given up on my hair and was now lying with her head in my lap. "I'm tired," she announced suddenly. "I want Morganne to put me to bed."

I took her inside the thatched-roof hut and made a cozy nest for her out of the soft animal-skin blankets. We curled up together, which is something I hadn't done with Tammy since she was a baby. Not that I remembered doing it, but my mom's favorite photo was of us sleeping together when we were younger. We looked awfully contented. The way things had been the past few years, you'd think that photo was faked.

The witch's riddles were floating around my head as I closed my eyes. Was it really my job to figure them out?

What's lost in the earth must be found.
But the earth must be turned without tilling. . . .

I relaxed and let sleep overtake me. Maybe when I woke up I'd be at Durty Nellie's puking my guts out, or in my bed at the inn with an ass-kicking hangover.

As I slipped off to dreamland, it calmed me to think I might wake up as buzz-cut Morgan again. Strange, considering how little I'd enjoyed being Morgan lately.

I'd miss Fergus, though. *Shame to waste a sweet guy like him on a swamp full of salamanders . . .*

thirteen

"Morganne, wake up!"

Ak.

It was still dark, I was in deep sleep, I was lying in a nest of animal-skin blankets, dreaming—

"Get up! We must go and watch! It's too funny!"

Erin was poking me and giggling madly. Evidently I was still Morganne in Long-ago Wheneverville, but no matter who I was it was much, much too early to wake up.

"What," I mumbled. I sat upright. My hair was a long red-gold tangle across my face. Erin parted it with her fingers like a curtain and whispered to me.

"It's almost dawn, and Fergus has gone to visit his beloved toad-lady. 'In the darkness before dawn is when she sings the sweetest,' he says. Come! We must see him woo her!"

Little sisters. Pains in the ass, wherever and whenever you

go. But the idea of spying on Fergus and his toad sounded pretty funny to me too.

"Awesome," I said, warming to our prank. "I wouldn't miss that for anything."

Erin said she knew the way to the swamp, but i thought it best to take Samhain. I didn't know how to ride a horse, but since I could tell Sam where to go I figured it would be more like taking a cab.

"Swamp, please!" I said, once Erin and I were on Sam's back. "And keep it quiet. We're trying to be discreet."

"I'll drop you a hundred paces away," snorted Sam. "You'll have to walk the rest of the way if you don't want to be heard."

"You can talk to Samhain?" Erin said, wide-eyed.

"Uh, sure." It hadn't occurred to me that everyone here in Long-ago couldn't. "Is that unusual or something?"

Erin laughed. "He's a *horse*, Morganne! Of course it's unusual!"

"But Fergus can too," I stammered. "Sorry, I just assumed—"

"Fergus can because he was given the gift of horse-language as a baby, when the Druids prophesied he would drive the chariot of the greatest hero in Ireland," Erin said, as we trotted along through the night. "But apart from Fergus, only those with faery blood can understand the speech of horses."

"Huh." Fergus had referred to the faeries as "your people," but I didn't know what he meant. Who were "my people," my parents, my family in this world?

There are an awful lot of things I can't remember about myself, I thought, but that made me think of the photo of me and baby Tammy, again.

On Samhain's back we'd left the dun and crossed a field full of sleepy cattle. The cows mooed in annoyance and ambled out of the way as we passed. Even in Long-ago the cows looked animatronic, like crudely mechanized heads attached to bodies made of painted carved wood—but that is what cows tend to look like, if you think about it. We reached the edge of a wood, where Sam slowed to a walk and picked his way carefully through the trees, over roots and stones and through low branches that made us cling tightly to his back.

Samhain stopped at the edge of a clearing. "I'll wait for you here," he said, tossing his head. "Be careful. The hour before sunrise is the night's last chance for mischief." I wondered what his voice sounded like to Erin. Snorting and whinnying, probably.

"I know where we are!" whispered Erin. "Follow me!"

Silently Erin led me through the clearing, through another small patch of trees, and then to the edge of the swamp. The water shimmered oddly, catching and reflecting the light of the moon.

Erin stopped and grabbed my arm. She put her fingers to her lips and pointed.

There, in the middle of the swamp, stretched out on a half-rotted log, was Fergus. His amphibious girlfriend was next to him, squatting on a lily pad and croaking her froggy little heart out.

"Say it again, my love!" Fergus's lovesick voice carried

over the water. "Tell me once more, that I may remember your words when we're apart!"

Croak. Croak.

"And I love you just as much, my darling." He stretched one hand out as if he would gently stroke the toad, but the log started to roll. "No, no, don't leap away from me again! Let me gaze upon your mottled beauty a precious moment more—"

The toad, startled by the movement of the log, hopped into the water—*plop!*—and disappeared. With a pained sigh Fergus started to paddle around the swamp, using the log as a flotation device.

"Brilliant!" whispered Erin. Her face was glowing with delight. "I want to get closer!" Before I could say anything she scampered off into the darkness. I could hear the crackle of her footsteps receding as she circled along the water's edge to the far end of the swamp.

"Wait!" I whispered, too late. I followed in the direction I thought she'd gone, but I didn't know the way and it was harder for someone my size to pass through the tangle of reeds and bushes she'd slipped through like an eel. I followed, one step at a time, using the contour of the swamp as my guide. After a minute or two I couldn't hear Erin's footsteps at all.

Fergus, meanwhile, had begun to sing. I wanted to find it funny, but all at once I was uneasy out there in the dark.

"Swim to me, my lady, my love,
Swim and paddle to meeeee—"

I heard another sound: a high, shrill whinny in the distance.

"Listen, my dear! The seahorses themselves are singing your praises!" Fergus was delirious with passion.

"Erin!" I yelled. I didn't care if Fergus heard me. "Erin! Where are you?" I moved as quickly as I could through the undergrowth. The sky was still dark and dotted with stars, but there was a strange glow in the distance. I wasn't used to being outdoors before dawn—did the sunrise always look like this?

"Who's there?" Fergus turned around so quickly he slipped off the log and into the murky waters. He splashed and burbled, completely covered in mud.

"It's me, Fergus! It's Morganne." I said the name without thinking, as if it were my own. "We have to find Erin!"

"I'm here!" Erin's voice was playful and happy. "Don't worry, Morganne. I'm fine. And there's a boy here too." She sounded so close, but I couldn't see her.

Behind me I heard Fergus flailing about the shallow water, trying to crawl to dry land but slowed by the thick, sucking mud of the swamp.

"What boy?" I said, panicked. I turned in the direction of her voice and pushed my way through a high thicket of cattails. They whipped my face and got tangled in my hair as I thrashed my way to the unexpected clearing that lay beyond.

There was Erin, and there was the boy.

The glow I'd seen was not the sunrise at all. It was coming from the boy. He looked maybe twelve or so, slender and handsome and dressed in formal Victorian-style clothing, as if he'd just come from an elegant party many centuries from now. He gave off a soft, greenish light, and he was holding something out to Erin. She seemed transfixed.

"Don't touch that, Erin!" I used my meanest, sharpest big-sister voice. "Do. Not. Touch."

"Don't be silly, Morganne," Erin said, slowly. "It's only a peach. And I haven't had any breakfast."

Samhain's whinny cut through the air again. There was no mistaking the sound of alarm.

"Poor old nag," said the boy, turning his head and looking at me. A trail of brilliant, sparkling light followed his movements, then vanished, like the fading streaks of a meteor shower. The boy smiled. "He says you've been away too long, and it's time to go back. Morgan."

Fergus appeared next to me, caked in mud and slime. It took him only a split second to understand what was happening.

"What are you doing—Erin! *Stop!*"

But Erin was already taking a juicy, slow-motion bite of the peach. The boy smiled again and turned away from us. He took Erin's free hand.

A raw, bottomless crack in the ground opened up, and Erin and the boy sank into it, quickly and smoothly, as if they were riding a down escalator into the earth.

I leapt after her, with Fergus right beside me, reaching hard like I was sliding headfirst into home plate, stretching out my fingertips to grab hold of the crevice's lip before it closed completely. . . .

What's lost in the earth must be found. . . .

fourteen

My mouth was full of dirt.

That's what it tasted like. A foul, swamp-dirt taste, like how your mouth feels when you wake up with a skull-splitting hangover in a foreign country and can't remember how you got into bed or who cleaned up your puke.

"Erin," I tried to yell, but my voice was a croak.

Erin.

the day, the time—this information was not available to me. I stumbled to the bathroom and washed my face before I looked in the mirror.

I was Morgan. Green-faced and nearly hairless as a toad. My brain was pounding, and my eyes felt like they were being pushed out of their sockets. I could hardly turn my head.

The bottle of Advil was still open from when I'd used it

last. (Was that yesterday? Last week? Last year?) No pain-killers for me now. I needed to feel every scrap of misery and accursedness.

I couldn't afford to get comfortable. I had to get back and find Erin.

In the lobby of Durty Nellie's the entire merry padded-ass band of travelers was already gathered to receive their maps and instructions for the day. Lucia, actually smiling, was finishing some sort of story.

"Because we argued like an old married couple from the moment that we met, that's how we knew!" Everyone laughed.

"He sounds like a king of men," Heidi said, wiping away a little tear.

"I think you mean 'prince among men,'" corrected Lucia. "But Jack always treated me like a queen, believe me!"

When the group saw me they started whooping and ap-plauding. The sound rolled into my ears and bitch-slapped my brain around my skull until I grabbed the back of a sofa for support.

"If it isn't the toast of the town!" Patty laughed, slapping me on the back. "I've a mind to cancel the bike tour today so the village can have a parade in your honor!"

What? I couldn't have heard her right. Something about a parade—must have been some fascinating historic tidbit about the village's annual potato parade or something—

"Good times, good times," said Stuart with a sigh. He and Carrie both had their sunglasses on, even though we were still indoors. "What a night. I haven't partied that hard since Sundance."

"What happened?" asked Sophie Billingsley, bouncing up and down. "Was there a party? Why wasn't I invited?"

"Because it wasn't for *babies*," sneered Derek.

"There wasn't any party, dear," soothed Mrs. Billingsley. She stroked her daughter's hair and looked at her husband with concern. "Was there?"

Mr. Billingsley shoved his hands in his pockets. "Other than young Morgan here drinking half the men in the pub under the table and dancing the legs off the chaps left standing, no, I wouldn't say so," he said with an embarrassed chuckle. "Didn't see it firsthand, of course, I don't go in for that sort of carousing." He glanced at me and looked away. "But it was all the talk at breakfast."

"You were fantastic!" Heidi beamed. "American girls are so inner get ick!" She meant *energetic,* I figured out after a second. "Inner get ick! They'll do anything! That's what Johannes says." Johannes turned vividly red.

Lucy Faraday gave me a hug. "I'm so glad you're feeling better," she said.

"Thanks," I said, trying not to panic.

So. Evidently some stuff happened the previous night. So what. I was hardly the first person to get wasted and not remember all the gory details the next day. It sounded like no harm was done, except maybe to my liver.

At least only one night has passed, I thought. One night here, one night in Long-ago. Maybe the time zones had gotten lined up somehow.

Sophie's bouncing up and down was making my head

throb, but it also made me think of Erin. Where was she? How was I supposed to get back to Long-ago and save her?

The faery boy had called me Morgan. Strange.

I turned to Patty. "If it's okay, I'm gonna ride in the van today," I said, trying to sound weak and pathetic. It wasn't hard. "I have a really stiff neck."

"After last night I'm surprised you can walk!" said Patty. "Don't worry. We'll have Colin load your bike into the van. And I'm sure *he'll* welcome your company."

Was there an edge of insinuation in her voice? Hard to tell. How did Colin figure into my night of carousing? This not knowing what I'd done and who I'd done it with was very unnerving.

"You'll be needing this I'm sure," Patty said, as she handed me a strong cup of Irish tea. She winked at me, as these Irish people seemed to do so well. "I'd wager you have some Irish blood in you, don't you?"

"I think I must," I said.

Colin was jolly like he always was, whistling and goofing around as he put my bike in the back of the van with the luggage—but he seemed to be doing it all a little bit more inner-get-ickally than usual. He was hyped up for some reason. Was I the reason?

I figured since I couldn't remember any of what happened the night before, the best defense was a good offense. After we'd been driving along for some time and my head and stomach had adjusted to the bumping and lurching of the van, I made my move.

"I had a great time last night," I said. What the hell, right? He grinned. "Me too."

We drove. Okay, that got me exactly nowhere.

Those American girls will do anything. Gag. Not with Johannes, I hope. But what had I done with Colin? Anything more than dancing? That would be something I'd want to remember.

Colin drummed his fingers on the steering wheel in a happy-go-lucky way. "You're a marvelous girl when you let your spirits loose, Mor," he said, after a while. "I figured you were, you know, but it was good to finally see it with my own eyes."

"Colin, look." I was staring out the window.

"What? That?" He looked and then laughed. "What's the matter, lass, haven't you ever seen a rainbow before?"

"Not like that," I said, dumbfounded. Connecticut didn't get too many rainbows, it's true, but even I could tell that what I was looking at was not purely a weather phenomenon. This rainbow was shimmering, sparkling, bathed in a fine mist of slowly falling glitter. It looked like one of those tacky animated MySpace graphics.

"It rains a great deal in Ireland, so the rainbows are never far behind," he said, matter-of-factly. "We get accustomed to them."

"But," I stammered. "But Colin. *Look.*"

"Oh, they're pretty, make no mistake. It's just water droplets, you know. The light refracts through the atmosphere and the water acts as a prism. . . ."

Colin, professional tour guide that he was, proceeded to give me a very boring explanation of how rainbows are formed. It was obvious that he and I were not looking at the same rainbow.

Strange.

I must be very close, I thought. Very close to being able to slip back to Long-ago. But how?

"Did you mean what you said last night, Mor? About tonight?"

Poor me, with no clue what I'd said. And poor Colin, sounding so hopeful. Luckily I had a pretty good BS reflex (thanks Mom, thanks Dad).

"I usually do," I said, carefully neutral.

"Fine. Fine." He seemed quite satisfied. "We'll have a marvelous time, then."

Plans had been forged and promises made, and I had no idea what they were. Under different circumstances I'd be tingly at the prospect of having something going on with Colin tonight, even if I didn't know exactly what it was. But right now Erin was all I could think about. I needed to concentrate.

"Would you mind," I said, "if I took a nap?"

He smiled. "Not if I get to watch you sleep."

I closed my eyes.

What's lost in the earth must be found. . . .

How was I supposed to get back to Long-ago to find Erin?

How had it happened before? I whacked my head on a rock. I drank till I passed out. There was definitely a pattern here. All I had to do was get myself totally fekked up somehow and the doorway to Long-ago swung open.

Some vacation this was turning out to be. The thought of more drinking made my stomach lurch. But if that's what it took, that's what I'd do.

Because Erin needed me, and she was real. Fergus, too, and Cúchulainn and Samhain and all the rest. They were as real as I was, and just because I couldn't see them at the moment and they lived in the past didn't mean squat. They were real, the way my family and friends in Connecticut were real, even though they were across the ocean and five hours in the past, from a Greenwich Mean Time perspective.

The way those long-ago versions of me and Tammy in that old photo were real, even though I couldn't remember it.

The way Jack Faraday was real, and always would be, even though he was dead.

Even the way Colin's dreams of what he might be someday were real, even though no one could see those dreams but him.

Poor Fergus. He must be crazed. I hoped he and Cúchulainn weren't randomly galloping through the countryside lopping off heads and limbs just because they were pissed off. That kind of display was unlikely to make much of an impression on the faery folk. That much I understood by now.

I had to get back.

Think, Morgan, I told myself. *You are an inner-get-ick American high-school girl, and if you don't know how to get yourself fekked up you have just not been paying attention.*

I thought of the most reckless kids I knew and made my list. Beer, always an option, though at the moment a highly unappetizing one. Dropping E was another party favorite, but it scared me (I was no druggie), plus, duh, I didn't have any. Sleep deprivation? Possible but very difficult. I had a really hard time staying awake when I was tired, as had been proven by many failed attempts to cram for tests or write lengthy papers the night before they were due.

What else? There'd been a cheerleader in my freshman class who stopped eating for a couple of months until she got delirious and was shipped off to eating disorder rehab, but I didn't have that kind of time. And Raph used to talk about a "runner's high" that kicked in when he was training. Usually you had to be running at a good clip for forty minutes or so before you felt it.

Me, run for forty minutes? Yeah, right. I'd hardly exercised at all since my field hockey days. I'd be lucky to run to the corner.

As we drove, the rainbow followed us the way the moon follows you when you walk at night. I knew what it was telling me.

It was up to me—Morganne, Morgan, all of me. It was my job to find Erin. And if I didn't, no one would.

. . . but the earth must be turned without tilling. . . .

As we drove I napped, I dozed, I chanted in my head using my mom's old meditation mantra. I held my breath until I felt dizzy. Anything to alter my brain waves. But nothing happened.

When that got old I entertained myself by making up personal ads for King Conor.

I'LL TREAT YOU LIKE A QUEEN. . . .

Party-loving monarch seeks special fire-and-gold someone for breaking curses and sharing good times.
Equally comfortable in crown and scepter, tuxedo or
jeans.

When I dozed I dreamed, but they were actual dreamlike
dreams: snatches of home, school, stuff from when I was a
little kid, my favorite bits from *Scary Movie 4*, all random and
jumbled the way dreams are supposed to be. No sign of a
portal to other times and places. At the moment I was travel-
ing nowhere except to where Colin was driving me.

I startled awake to the sound of a teeny, tiny heavy metal
band playing its heart out through a kazoo. It was Colin's cell
phone.

"Nice ring, eh?" he said, as he grabbed the phone from his
shirt pocket. "I'm a big fan of the death metal—Colin here!
Yes. Right. Ah, that's a pity. Where are you now, then?" He
looked at his watch. "Right, not to worry, we'll do our best.
Take a few deep breaths, dear. It'll calm you down. Cheers."

"Fek it," he said, flipping his phone shut. "Pardon the language, Mor. We have to go fetch Miss Pippin."

"Why? Did she get hurt? Did she break a nail?" I yawned
and stretched. "Did her implants deflate?"

Colin sighed. "I'm afraid it's worse than that."

"*let me impress upon you. It is a borrowed ear-*
ring. It is from Harry *Winston*." For a woman who was little

more than skin and bones and silicone, Carrie Pippin sure could produce a lot of sound. She covered her face with her manicured hands in an impressive gesture of despair. "Do you *know* who Harry Winston is?"

"Haven't met him, sorry," said Colin, staring at the ground. "It's round, you said? Like a hoop?"

Colin and Stuart and I were scanning the road searching for a single, obscenely expensive hoop earring whose twin was on Carrie Pippin's left ear. She was much too hysterical to join the search and kept touching the remaining earring as if it might vaporize at any moment.

"We're never gonna find it, babe," Stuart said, helpfully. "We've been riding the bikes for an hour. You could have lost it anywhere in the last ten miles."

Carrie's already strident voice climbed higher and higher as she spoke. "Would you *stop* being so *negative*! I'm sure I would have noticed earlier if it were gone. For God's sake, it's a *Harry Winston*! You *notice* when something like that falls off!"

"Whoa, I think I see it!" hollered Colin. He squatted and dug around in the dirt. "Whoops! Bottle cap. Sorry, false alarm."

"Maybe it's turned into faery gold," Stuart said. "Some old coot was telling me about that this morning when I was trying to buy the paper. Do you know how difficult it is to find a copy of *Variety* in this country? *The Hollywood Reporter*? I would've settled for the *LA Times*!"

"What's faery gold?" I asked. Colin rolled his eyes.

"It's when you see gold on the ground but every time you try to pick it up it turns to dust . . . just like show business, ha ha!"

At that Carrie started crying, and Stuart stopped his half-hearted searching to go comfort her. I could hear her blubbering on and on.

". . . they were nice enough to lend it for my honeymoon and *this* happens. . . . Now what am I going to do for the Emmys? . . . Maybe we can call someone at Bulgari—oh my God, if Bulgari finds out about this I'll be *blacklisted*. . . ."

What an idiot, I thought. Here I was, looking for some stupid earring when I was supposed to be searching for Erin. And my head still hurt, and despite all the talk about the rainy Irish weather the sun's glare was making my eyes water, and bending over to search the ground was not doing wonders for my hangover either.

I spotted another bottle cap in the dirt. I'd never been much of a do-gooder, especially when it came to picking up other people's trash, but the roads here were so spotless it made even a tiny bit of litter seem disgusting. I'd put the cap in the garbage; then at least some good would come of this ridiculous search.

I brushed the dirt away from the metal and was blinded for a second, as sun glinted off the pure gold and directly into my eyes. It was a gleaming gold circle, the size of a bracelet. Without thinking I stuck my hand through it.

"Do you like it? I'll give you a good price."

"I don't have any money," I heard myself say. My voice was slow and warped-sounding, as if I were underwater.

"Come, dear, you must have *some* money. I'll take half of what it's worth. You were meant to have it. Look how it matches your hair."

My hair. Long and flowing, the color of fire and gold.

* * *

the long-ago marketplace where i'd suddenly found myself was wall-to-wall people, pushing, pointing, haggling, buying. There were heaping baskets everywhere of fruit, vegetables, cheese, eggs, fish and stuff you'd never find at Lucky Lou's: animal skins, armor, weapons and, in front me, jewelry.

The jewelry seller was a sharp-featured woman, slender and dark, Italian-looking, really, and roughly middle-aged (though it was hard to tell with these Long-ago people, who spent most of their days outdoors with no access to sunscreen and teeth whiteners and plastic surgeons). The woman had bracelets up and down her arms, dozens of necklaces draped around her neck and rings on every finger.

"That's a lot of bling," I heard myself say.

"I make it all myself," she boasted, grabbing my hand and lifting my wrist up until the bracelet caught the sunlight. "See? Pure gold! Melted in the furnace that was my father's. Show me another woman skilled as I am in forging metal into such beauty as you see here!"

"Morganne!"

Fergus was here. I saw him bobbing up and down in the throngs of people, waving and calling to me. I wanted to go to him but I didn't seem to be able to move. I could only watch as he pushed his way through the crowd to where I was. People pushed back but he didn't draw his sword once. I knew this took real restraint on his part.

"Ah, never mind about the money!" said the woman, following my gaze. "Your husband will pay. How could he refuse when he sees how it flatters your beauty?"

"Morganne! Are you truly here? Or just a vision?"

Fergus's voice sounded oddly warped, like my own. I had the feeling I was only half-present in Long-ago, but the jewelry maker was still hanging on to my arm and that felt real enough.

No time even for hello. "Has Erin come back?" I demanded to know.

His face fell. "No."

"How long has it been?"

"Almost two weeks," he said, confused. "But you know that—you were there at the swamp—right before you disappeared again—"

"Of course I know it's not the *original* Spago! I meant the one in Beverly Hills. . . ."

Carrie's voice was buzzing in my ear like a fly, coming from somewhere not too far away. I felt myself slipping back. "Fergus, listen," I said. "I can't stay long. But this woman—"

He waved dismissively. "She's just a conniving merchant; don't pay her any mind," he said.

"No, *look*." I grabbed his hand and made him touch the bracelet on my arm. "Fire and gold. That's how this was made. She forged it out of fire and gold. It's her."

He stared at the leering, blinged-out jewelry maker. She grinned and there was a glint of gold on one of her teeth.

"Her?" he said, horrified. "*She's* the one who has to marry the king?"

"Equally comfortable in scepter or jeans," I babbled. "But

she has to be willing, so don't say anything to freak her out, okay?" My vision swirled, and I knew I wasn't making sense. "Sorry, I gotta go, Fergus" I said. "But don't worry. I'll be back. I'll find her. I'll find—"

"Morgan!" screeched Carrie, who was clutching my arm hard enough to make little white fingerprints on my skin.

I held my wrist out so she could slide the earring off.

"I found it," I said, dumbly.

"Oh my God! *Oh my God!* I *love* you! You *saved* my *ass*! If you ever come to LA I am *so* taking you to Spago for lunch, you fabulous, brilliant person you!"

But I hadn't found what I was looking for. Not yet.

fifteen

plucking Carrie's earring out of the dirt, golden-needle-in-Irish-haystack style, only added to my growing legend among my tour mates. At dinner Sophie Billingsley asked me if I was magic. I just smiled and helped cut her steak. Her mother was not at the table; apparently Mrs. Billingsley was having some kind of digestive upset and was in her room, with her husband taking care of her.

I'd volunteered to mind Sophie and Derek at dinner. Why not? They both acted much more pleasant when their parents weren't around.

"Did you know," Sophie confided, as I squeezed more ketchup onto her plate, "that I can see faeries?"

"Really," I said. Tammy said stuff like this all the time. I guess I should have paid more attention. "Where do you see them?"

"Everywhere!" she said. "Well, in flower gardens, mostly.

And where mushrooms grow. But soon I'll be too old," she added, sadly. "Like Derek."

"Too old for what?"

"To see them. That's what they tell me, anyway."

"Well, I'm not too old to see them," I said. "So you won't ever be either."

She had to think about that for a minute. "That's fine, then," she finally said, serenely. "Will you play with me later? After dinner?"

I looked across the table at Colin. He was listening kindly to Lucia, who'd gotten much more talkative today. "That would be great, Sophie. But I promised Colin I was doing something with him after dinner."

"What?"

"I don't know," I answered truthfully. "But I promised, and a promise is a promise."

"It won't be as fun as the faeries," she said, stuffing a last bite into her mouth. Then she ran outside to join Derek and Johannes. Johannes had offered to give the kids horsy rides on his back. I could hear him whinnying and neighing. Quite convincing, really.

As it turned out, what I'd promised Colin was to go skinny-dipping at the beach after dark. He parked the van in the near-empty lot, and I breathed in the familiar salt tang of the sea.

Growing up in Connecticut not far from the coast meant I'd had plenty of beach time in my life. Family beach trips with Mom and Dad and Tammy, gang-of-girlfriend beach trips with Sarah and our old crowd, nighttime make-out beach excursions with Raph and his entourage. Raph was a big one for the beach and for making out, but he never went anywhere without his posse. They'd leave empty beer bottles on the sand and have peeing contests in the water: Who could pee furthest, longest, highest. Classy, right?

I'd gone with them, of course, even though I always ended up sitting there shivering and embarrassed. When Raph's buddies had girlfriends, the girlfriends would come too, but Raph *always* had a girlfriend. Before me it was this girl named Stephanie. She was a junior like Raph so I didn't really know her, I just knew who she was.

"Too bossy." That's what Raph had told me about Stephanie. "Too stubborn."

By now—mid-July—the Connecticut beaches would be packed, the water would be warm. Colin and I were on this side of the Atlantic, Raph was on the other. Maybe it was because I had a lot on my mind, but at the moment I didn't really care who Raph was with. That surprised me, a little.

"People think of surfing and they think of hawaii," Colin said, as we walked along the sand. He had a blanket and two towels tossed over one shoulder, and he was talking in his high-energy tour-guide voice. "But Ireland has some of the finest beaches you'll find anywhere. Just had the national wind-surfing championships right here in Elly Bay. Rained the whole fekkin' time of course. Which is why," and he looked at me to make sure I was being sufficiently entertained by his monologue, "people think of Hawaii."

The beach was beautiful, moonlit and nearly empty. And I would have been entertained, charmed, swooning with happiness even, if I wasn't brooding on how to get back to Longago and find Erin.

I wished I could tell Colin why I wasn't bubbling over with delight and flirtiness. *A cruel irony* is what Sarah would have called it: me, an adorable and interested guy (with an accent no less), on an after-hours beach date that should have been a perfect summer-romance moment. And I was distracted, faking my way through as best I could because my mind was a million miles away.

Scratch that. My mind was right here. Just a few thousand years off schedule.

Should I tell Colin what was going on? He deserved to know why I was being so distant, and I was dying to confide in anyone who could help me figure out what kind of alternate universe I'd been head-whacked into. But Colin was a passionate nonbeliever in things magical and mystical. Would my time-warped tale spoil whatever attraction he was starting to feel for me and convince him to take me back to the hospital, the psych ward this time?

Probably. But like a moth dive-bombing into a neon sign that read MOTHS DIE HERE, I couldn't seem to stop myself from finding out.

"Colin," I said, as he smoothed the sand with his bare feet to make a spot for us. "There's been something I've been wanting to tell you, but I haven't, because I don't know how you're going to react."

"Let me guess," he said, as he shook out the blanket he'd swiped from the inn. I caught the far corners in midair.

"You've got a boyfriend at home, and you both agreed what happens in Ireland stays in Ireland, but you thought I should know on the chance I was dumb enough to think you actually fancied me—that sort of thing?"

I was shocked. "Of course not!" I said. We both sank to our knees in the sand while holding on to the edges of the blanket, which floated down slowly, like a tired parachute. "That's gross. Is that what you thought I was going to say?"

He brushed the sand off his legs, sat on the blanket and shrugged. "Doing what I do, I meet girls from all over the world. Some of them consider it part of the holiday, bagging some local action before going home to the hubby. Bit of a souvenir, you know?" Colin looked out at the dark water, away from me. For once the cheerful tone of his voice seemed forced. "You learn the hard way not to get too attached."

I was glad he couldn't see my face, because *rebound souvenir* is more or less exactly how I'd pegged Colin when I first met him. But that was two very long days ago, and what I'd felt then and what I was feeling now were as different as earth and water, fire and gold. I liked Colin, I knew I did. But there was an awful lot I hadn't told him.

"I don't have a boyfriend," I answered, as we both sat there looking out at the water. "I really don't, Colin."

Hearing myself say it was like casting a spell that made it, finally, true. *Aloha, Raph,* I thought, probably because Colin had mentioned Hawaii before. It was midafternoon in Connecticut, a lovely time for a swim.

For a long while all we could hear was the rhythmic whooshing of the sea and the high screech of the seagulls. *No, Colin, I don't have a boyfriend, but there is this hunky warrior-dude*

I like, mostly because he looks a lot like you, but don't sweat it because by now he's been dead for thousands of years. . . .

"No boyfriend, eh? That's lucky for me, then," Colin said, softly. "But then again, I tend to be a very lucky person."

I was about to ask him how he could believe in luck when he didn't believe in magic or faeries, but then I thought I'd be better off trying to improve my own luck. So I kissed him instead.

but the earth must be turned without tilling. . . .

Soon we were so breathless and crazed from making out that we stopped, because if we didn't stop we wouldn't have, and this was much too sweet to let happen so fast.

I even temporarily forgot about my other self, my other world, the life-and-death responsibility that was waiting for me in a place I had no idea how to get back to. That's the kind of kisser Colin was. The kind that makes you forget everything else till your toes wiggle with electric shocks of pleasure and your civilized human brain shuts down completely, leaving only the primal lizard make-out brain in charge. We were lying next to each other on the blanket now, and I was touching him without even knowing that I was.

"Have a little mercy, there, darling," he said, moving my hand to safer ground. "I'm a healthy young bloke and the management cannot be held responsible if you leave your possessions unattended."

I cracked up. "What does that mean?"

"It means my luck seems to be holding up." He snickered, Groucho Marx style. "Well up."

"Luck?" I murmured, arching myself close enough to him

that I could feel the heat of his body again. "I thought you didn't believe in that kind of stuff."

"Just because I think Ireland should join the twenty-first century does not mean I'm a complete prig, Miss!" he said, propping his head up on his hand and grinning down at me. "I've been known to play the lottery. I read my horoscope like the next man."

He brushed his lips across the top of my head. "Soft as a peach," he whispered. "Just like you, Mor. You're a peach yourself, aren't you? One thing on the outside, something completely different, softer and sweeter, underneath."

Erin. I thought of Erin eating the peach. Where was she now?

My hands were safely stowed, but one of Colin's had crept under the bottom of my shirt, as he talked quiet music in my ear.

"I used to fancy a bit of Asian mysticism, to tell you the truth," he said, as his hand slowly made its way north across my tummy. "The I Ching. Reading tea leaves. Numerology was a particular favorite; it appeals to the engineer in me." He took one of my earlobes gently in his teeth, and his fingertips wandered up another inch, and for all the euros in Ireland I could not have told you my own name at that moment.

"Let's do you," he said, and for a moment I misunderstood. "Date of birth?

"June third," I whispered. The weight and warmth of his hand on my skin was making my heart race, the earth spin—

"Ah, a Gemini," he said. "That means there's two of you, but we knew that already! June third. So we've got six and three, now add in the year—"

"Nineteen-ninety-one," I purred, without thinking. Believe me, there was no thinking at all going on at that moment.

Colin's hand froze in place exactly where it was.

"Bloody *hell,* girl, are you sixteen years old?"

Oh, fek.

"Colin, don't be mad, please—"

He sat up and moved about two feet away from me, but it might as well have been a mile.

"*Why* for fek's sake would you lie about a thing like that?"

"I didn't want you to think I was a kid!"

"But you *are* a bloody kid, aren't you?" Colin was yelling at me like he'd caught me sticking gum under the table. "What sort of bloke do you take me for? I'm not a bloody child molester."

It was like someone had suddenly turned a glaringly bright light on us, but of course no one had. We were alone and the night was as dark as ever. "Why is eighteen so different from sixteen?" I asked stubbornly.

"Because it just bloody is, all right? And me buying you drinks in the pub! They should haul me off in irons."

I didn't say anything, and Colin realized I was crying.

"Now, now, there, there. I'm not mad at you."

"Yes, you are." I sniffed.

"Well, yes I am! But I'll get over it." He had his hands on his knees, trying to be completely stern with me and not entirely succeeding. "Just tell me—what were you thinking, Morgan—do you think this sorta thing is a joke? Or are you some type of psychopath that I should know about?"

"No," I said, laughing a little through my tears. "I only

lied because I like you and I wanted to—I wanted you to—"

"Right." He rubbed his head with both hands till his hair stood up at crazy angles. "Listen to me now; this is important. It's when you like people that you should be most willin' to tell 'em the truth about yourself."

Easy for him to say. "Does this mean you're not attracted to me anymore?"

"Not attracted to you?" Colin sputtered. "Are you insane? I'm practically baying at the moon, here—I'd eat you up like a bowl of pudding if I could! Get up."

He leapt to his feet and grabbed my wrist.

"Hey!" I protested, as he started dragging me across the sand to the water. "What are you doing?"

"We're going swimming."

"But I still have my clothes on!"

"And you shall keep them on, young lady!"

"But I didn't bring anything else to—Colin! No, it's freezing!" A wave had swirled around our ankles, and the water was so cold it made me jump.

He looked at me with a helpless expression. "That's why we're going swimming. Now *in*!"

Once we were completely wet the icy water turned bearable, then comfortable, until we were diving and splashing and chasing each other underwater like dolphins. It was dark enough that I would lose track of where the surface was while I was swimming below. The only way back was to relax and let the salt water lift me till I bobbed up to the air, and the moonlight and stars reappeared.

"Have you cooled off yet, you underage temptress? You teenage siren?" Colin said, blowing water out of his nose.

"Yes," I said. "I've completely lost interest in you. Colin who? Some old man I met on vacation."

"Good. Because when we get back to the inn"—he panted, as the water dripped down his face—"I'm booking you on a tour two summers from now—"

"No way!" I cried, splashing him. "Not another bike tour!"

"Two summers from now, when you're eighteen," he went on, splashing me right back. "And I promise you, it'll be the best vacation of your—"

"Shark attack!" I yelled, diving underneath and kicking hard toward him, my hands reaching out to grab his leg. He moved, but too slowly, and we tumbled and turned under the water. I let go of him and relaxed so I could rise to the surface again. I felt myself floating up and opened my eyes.

It wasn't starlight or moonlight, but there was some kind of light, and it was getting closer. And I was still underwater. I felt a gentle pulling sensation behind me, as if I'd gotten tangled in a long mass of seaweed. I shook my head to get loose of it, but I couldn't.

The light got closer still. I knew I should be panicking, running out of air, scrambling to find the surface. But I wasn't. I was fine.

I spun around to see if I could find Colin. Instead I saw my own hair, floating like an amber cloud around my head.

"Welcome, Morganne, to the land of the merrows," said a gentle, melodious voice. The murk of the water in front of me got brighter and brighter until I saw a woman's face suddenly appear, greenish and beautiful and emanating light.

There were so many questions I could ask. *Where's Colin? Why am I not running out of air? Who the fek are you, green water woman?* But instead I said:

"What's a merrow?"

"I think you call us 'mermaids.'" She smiled. Her teeth were whorled like seashells. "I can show you where the little girl is. But you have to come with me. *Now*."

The merrow kicked her fishy feet and swam off, and without hesitation I followed her out to sea, leaving Colin and the shore far, far behind.

sixteen

i went to ireland on vacation and all i got was this lousy pair of gills.

Okay, not very original. How about this:

Just go with it.

There. My new motto. I could have a T-shirt made at the mall when I got home.

I swam after the merrow, deeper into the ocean. Erin was out there somewhere, and this is how I was going to get her back.

I hadn't breathed the air in hours, it felt like.

Just go with it.

i wish i could describe a technicolor disney kingdom of happy animated water creatures singing rhymed ditties to a Jamaican beat. *Little Fekkin' Mermaid* was one of

Tammy's all-time favorite movies, and the fact that she had to watch it at full volume seven times a day for an entire year was one of the formative events leading to my hatred of the open-plan-house school of suburban architecture.

"Just put the TV in her rooooooommmmm!!!!" I'd screamed at my mother.

"You know we don't believe in kids having TVs in their rooms," she'd replied, sweetly ignoring my tantrum. "It has a lot of negative effects." Her and her parenting magazines.

"But now we ALL have the TV in our room!" I yelled back. "This house is one big room and Tammy gets to watch the TV and I'm suffering the negative effects! Get it?"

My mom sighed.

"You were a little girl once too, Morgan. I wish you could be more understanding."

If I ever get home to tell Tammy about this, I'll lie, I thought, as I swam through the cold murk pursuing a naked green woman who might be leading me to my doom. I'd tell Tammy it was exactly like a Disney movie. There were beautiful animated girls with seashell combs in their hair, and the fish were cracking jokes like Nemo, and we would all periodically break into big dance numbers while singing peppy songs.

That would make her so happy.

We'd swum at least halfway to Connecticut, it felt like, when the merrow turned and gestured to me with her long webbed fingers.

She gestured downward.

To the ocean floor.

I thought of Leonardo DiCaprio in *Titanic*, dead at the bottom of the sea. I thought of the exhibit at the Museum of Natural History, where the titans of the deep fight to the death, the giant squid versus the killer whale. My money was always on the squid. It just looked meaner.

What would I have to do to get Erin back?

Down we dove.

every scrap of science class that i could muster back into memory was telling me I should be dead, suffocated, smooshed by the water pressure or getting the bends. Or did that only happen on the way up?

But instead we swam down, down, me following the shimmering green light of the merrow through the relentless darkness of the sea. After what felt like miles of descent a massive cliff loomed in front of us, its huge bulk suddenly visible in the ghostly merrow-light. How high the cliff was and how far we were from the ocean floor I couldn't say, but there was a cliff and we headed toward it.

The merrow looked back to see if I was still there. When she saw me she smiled. Then she gave an extra kick (she didn't have a fish tail like a Disney mermaid, by the way—just long and very powerful-looking legs, green of course, and flattish webbed feet), and zipped over to the cliff. There, she pulled away a gently pulsing curtain of seaweed to reveal what looked like the entrance to a cave. She gestured for me to go inside.

Tammy would not have been disappointed. Through the

narrow cave entrance in the cliff lay an entire world—a dry and sunny one. The dark ocean water remained outside, held back by some invisible force like the walls of the Red Sea in *The Ten Commandments* (which my parents used to make us watch every Easter, not for any religious reason but so Tammy and I would appreciate how far movie special effects have come since then).

Stepping through the cave entrance was like stepping out of a cold shower and finding myself under a warm sunlamp. Where did the light come from? Where did the *air* come from? Important questions, but I had a more important one to ask.

"Okay, we're here," I said to my green guide. "Where's the little girl?"

The merrow flashed her gnarly-toothed smile at me once more. For the first time I noticed that she wasn't completely naked, though the private parts of her definitely were (like all boobs, hers had been highly flotational while we were swimming, but now that they weren't suspended by seawater I could see that flotational was their permanent position—a bit unnatural, but how natural can you expect green boobs to look?). On her head, the merrow was wearing a little red hat, made out of—of all things—feathers.

"You'll have to speak to the king," she said, with some effort. Those teeth needed work. "Here he comes."

She bowed down low, letting her long mossy hair trail on the ground. In my sopping princess outfit I felt like an overdressed contestant in a wet T-shirt contest, but at least I wasn't naked.

This was not much comfort, though, because the king *was* naked. So were the other fifty merrow-people who showed up with him. Apparently I was at the underwater merrow nudist colony. This wouldn't have been so bad if they were all lovely green people like my barnacle-toothed escort, but the guy merrows were hideous, like a genetic cross between an ugly human being and a grouper.

The naked fish-king stood there looking at me, and I finally composed myself enough to give a little curtsey. That seemed to satisfy his royal ego enough for the conversation to begin.

"Bring out the girl!" he proclaimed, in a very kinglike fashion.

Two green women brought Erin forward. I was relieved to see that she was still wearing her dress. When she saw me she grinned, but I shushed her with a look before she had a chance to start carrying on like an overexcited kid. I had a feeling the merrows weren't going to just hand her over.

"Now tell me, Half-Goddess from the Land Beyond the Edge of the Sea!" said the king. "Have the terms of the enchantment been fulfilled?"

"Absolutely," I said. I had no idea what he was talking about, but if he thought I was some kind of enchantment-fulfilling half-goddess, I could totally work with that.

"How was the enchantment fulfilled?" asked the king.

I'd have to bluff, but I wasn't worried. When it comes to BS I knew I had a talent. We're talking about someone who made it all the way through Mrs. McKinney's chemistry class without ever figuring out what the periodic table was. With a B-minus average, thank you.

"It just was," I answered, the picture of confidence. "That's all you need to know."

There was a general whispering and hubbub, and the

king's chief flunky (even naked, you could tell which one he was) whispered something in the royal ear.

"Apparently you would not be here unless the terms of the enchantment had been fulfilled," the king explained, sounding disappointed. "But in order to release the girl, we do need the pertinent details. There are forms to fill out and such. Unless there has been some mistake? Can someone repeat the enchantment, please?"

One of the king's lesser flunkies unfurled a long scroll (poor guy had to carry it everywhere, I guess, what with no pockets available in his merrow birthday suit). He read:

"What's lost in the earth must be found,
"But the earth must be turned without tilling."

"Ring any bells?" the king asked darkly. I could see he was getting antsy.

I concentrated hard on the riddle. "Well," I said, "there was this earring, from Harry Winston? And it was lost in the dirt and everyone was looking for it but for some reason I was the one to find it. Does that help?"

"Harry Winston!" bellowed the king to his flunky in charge of filling out forms. "Write it down! And?"

Think, Morgan. Erin was the other thing that was lost in the earth. And now she was found. So the earth must have been turned. But how?

Of course the earth turned; it turned every day. But who knew that in this pre-Galileo world? This was something different.

Think think think. What happened right before the merrow appeared? What altered my brain waves and broke the enchantment and brought me here? *Feel the earth, turning and moving and spinning, as you lay on the sand with Colin—*

"Yes!" I yelled. "It turned. It moved. It was amazing, frankly."

They seemed to know what I meant. The king looked at me with a raised eyebrow.

"Name?"

"Uh, Colin," I mumbled. I hoped Erin didn't hear me. The flunky wrote something down on the scroll.

"And yet you swear there was no tilling?" the king challenged.

"I'm sorry," I said meekly. "But what is tilling, exactly?"

The guy with the scroll cleared his throat. "Tilling. It's when the plough is pushed deeply into the life-giving soil. When the blade of the hoe pierces the warm and welcoming earth. When the farmer's tool plunges into the fertile field—"

"Nope," I said quickly. "There was none of that."

The king seemed skeptical. "But the earth turned?" he demanded again. "Are you sure?"

"Yes! God. Did it ever. And absolutely no tilling." I didn't want to get into any more details in front of Erin, but this time the chief flunky came to my assistance.

"Don't worry, your majesty," the fish-man said, loudly enough for Erin to hear. "If she's lying, they will not survive the trip back. The power of the enchantment will see to that."

"Indeed." The king scowled at me. I could see Erin's eyes grow wide with fear.

"Very well then. We will give you the girl," said the king. Without waiting another second, Erin raced to my side and wrapped her arms around my waist.

"But still," the king continued, "we must ask for something in return."

I have a nonrefundable Aer Lingus ticket to New York for a flight that leaves on Sunday, I thought. *And my enchantment-breaking services are pretty booked.* But I listened.

"One of our own kind is marooned on land. Foolish girl! She lent a fisherman her red cap, and now he refuses to return it unless she marries him and gives him all her sea treasure."

"What a jerk," I said sympathetically. "But can't she get herself another hat? You seem to have a lot of them." And in fact every one of the naked merrow-people was wearing a small red hat made of feathers, all identical except for the king's, which had a crownlike shape and a starfish perched festively on top.

They looked at me like I was stupid.

"Without our red caps, none of us can pass through the sea," explained the flunky. "We're not fish, you know."

Erin had her arms tightly around my waist. If they expected me to leave her here while I went shopping for a hat for this gullible mermaid—no way. I was taking Erin with me, no matter what.

"What is it I have to do?" I said, preparing to stand firm.

"All we need"—and now the king sounded humble—"is a lock of your hair."

My beautiful, waist-length, reddish-gold hair? Please. "You can have it all," I said. "Give me a scissor; I'll chop it off right now."

He held up a hand. "One lock will be sufficient to weave a cap that will bring her safely home. Besides, you will need the rest to secure your safe return through the waves," he said, "and that of your sister."

She wasn't my sister, of course, but whatever. With the sharpened edge of a piece of whalebone they sliced off a lock of my hair for their lost merrow and another that I braided tightly into Erin's wheat-colored hair.

"I wish I could see," Erin said, excited. "How do I look?" Tammy was the same way, always decorating her hair with little plastic bows and barrettes and dancing around in front of the mirror.

"Like a little mermaid," I said, and turned to the king. "Now how do we get home?"

He pointed straight ahead. Behind us was the cave entrance. Outside we could see the dark ocean water, held back by whatever magic kept this merrow-world dry at the bottom of the sea.

"Go back the way you came," he intoned. "Follow the green lady; she'll show you out."

We did as we were told, and the same stacked merrow who'd escorted me here led us back into the mouth of the cave. Erin stuck one finger into the wall of water and pulled it out quickly.

"Cold!" she said.

"Once you get in it's fine," I told her. I took her hand and held it tightly.

The green merrow pointed up.

"You're not coming?" I asked.

She shook her head and smiled and wiggled her webbed fingers.

"Ciao!" she said, and ran off.

"Do you know the way?" asked Erin, looking up at me with eyes full of trust and hero-worship.

"Sure," I said. Find our way back to dry land from the bottom of the middle of the ocean, and all without a map or an oxygen tank? Of course I could do that. Why not?

Still holding hands, Erin and I stepped out into the sea.

Going up was much easier than coming down.

"Relax," I said to Erin, as we gently kicked our feet. "The water will float us right to the top."

"Why?" she asked. Kids, always with the *why*.

"Because we're not as dense as the water, which makes us, um, buoyant or whatever—it just will, okay?"

She smiled and enjoyed the ride, but I was far more worried than I let on. The merrow had said up, but where would we surface? In the middle of the Atlantic? The Bermuda triangle? A backyard pool in Connecticut? The possibilities seemed pretty random.

Just go with it, I reminded myself. *It's gotten you this far.*

And I made a mental note to thank Colin, if I ever saw him again, for his role in breaking the enchantment. If he'd been a less spectacular kisser or a less decent guy—

"Look!" Erin pointed. There was light above us.

We kicked harder. The water seemed to get thicker and dirtier as we approached the surface. We both broke through to the air at the same time.

We were in the swamp. The same swamp where Erin had disappeared and Fergus had wooed his frog-love and where he always waited for the moment of enchantment to strike him so he wouldn't harass any tender-hearted human women with his uncontrollable passion.

Wouldn't it be really awesome luck, I thought, dreamily, if we had somehow fast-forwarded to the night of the new moon and Fergus was right here in the swamp, waiting to fall in love with the first female creature he sees when the first star appears in the sky? And here I come, popping out of the slime like a wet goddess flying out of a toaster, just in time to become the object of his hot 'n' heavy devotion—

"ERIN!" I screamed. "Hide! Get behind me!"

"What!" After managing that whole underwater journey so bravely, now I'd succeeded in making the poor girl terrified. "Why? What's the matter?"

"Because," I said, slowly scanning the swamp for signs of Fergus, "you don't want your own brother to fall in love with you, do you?"

"GROSS!"

Her little-girl voice could cut through your skull like a machete. A log moved. It raised its head and saw me, soggy and coated with slime. I pinned Erin tightly behind me.

"Morganne!" Fergus started to paddle toward us. Judging from how the fading rosy light was quickly turning to gray, the sun had recently set. "Any news of poor Erin? Is there any hope of finding her?"

"Fergus!" Erin yelled. "I'm a mermaid now!"

"Don't move!" I scolded her. "Stay right where you are."

Obediently Erin hid behind my dress, but I could feel her shaking with giggles.

"Is it really her?" Fergus cried, getting closer. "Is she safe? Where is she?"

I looked at the horizon. The last rays of light had disappeared beyond the hills.

"Look at me, Fergus," I ordered. "Erin is fine. Just look at me."

He glanced up at the sky too, which was growing darker by the minute.

"Morganne—" he said, realizing. "It's the night of the new moon—"

"Look at me," I demanded. I was not taking any chances. The poor kid had been through enough. "Don't look anywhere else. Just at me."

He did, and the first star of the night sky appeared. Fergus took in a sudden sharp breath and his voice got low.

"Oh, Mor." He sighed, reaching out to me. "Morganne, Morganne . . ."

He reached and reached, until he lost his balance and slipped off the log, right into the swamp. The water was so thick with glop his fall made more of a thud than a splash.

By the time Fergus climbed back to his feet, shook himself like a wet dog, embraced his wriggling sister and then put his muddy arms around me, Erin was laughing hysterically.

I would have laughed too but I couldn't. I was too busy being on the receiving end of Fergus's enchanted kiss.

And, just for the record, I didn't feel the least bit slutty making out with two different guys in one night. Partly this was because I was the half-goddess Morganne, and I kicked butt and swam oceans and could kiss whoever I wanted.

But mostly it was because Fergus's kiss was Colin's kiss too. I'd recognize it anywhere. It was magic.

seventeen

In long-ago, sixteen was plenty old enough for tilling. However, we were many, many centuries before the invention of CVS, and tilling without contraception could lead to some accidental, uh, harvests. It's true that my long hair did not travel back and forth with me from Long-ago to my own time, but the rest of me did, and I wasn't about to take that kind of chance.

Mom, Dad, guess what! I got knocked up by an ancient warrior-dude! No, you can't meet him, because he's been dead for thousands of years. But don't be surprised if the kid likes pulling the limbs off all his dolls.

No, thank you. There would be no tilling for me. Sigh.

I tried explaining all this to Fergus, but a man under an enchantment is not about to listen to reason. The more we talked about it the more he suffered and moaned and longed for me and the more irritated I became. After a while I started to see the wisdom in his I-only-date-salamanders plan, but it was too late for that now.

There were times with Raph when I'd imagine what it would be like to be with someone else. Someone who wasn't just hanging out with me because he liked having a girlfriend and my number had randomly come up.

Wouldn't it be amazing, I would think, *to find a guy who really, really loved me,* adored *me, fussed and fawned over me and made me feel like I was the center of his universe?*

I thought I would never be unhappy or lonely or critical of myself ever again, if I had someone like that in my life.

Now I did. And it was driving me nuts.

Wed fire and gold to the king,
But the lady herself must be willing. . . .

After the jewelry seller got over the initial shock of being kidnapped and dragged to the castle and told by a posse of shouting warriors that she had to marry King Conor *or else* (would it have been so hard to set the two of them up on a date and let nature take its course?), she started working the situation for all it was worth. Cúchulainn in particular had a very hard time understanding why she didn't just say yes.

"The man is a *king*! What more could she want?" he grumbled. "Why must she be feasted and wooed every hour? Have you heard her latest demands? She wants to postpone the wedding *again* because she feels they need to 'get to know each other better'! Have you ever heard of such madness?"

"She sounds like a woman ahead of her time," I said. I fed

another sprig of Queen Anne's lace into the mouth of a very cute little goat. All day long, Fergus had been running out to the fields and coming back with armloads of wildflowers for me. Erin and I had made the first dozen batches into floral arrangements, wreaths, swags, headpieces and everything else we could think of, but then I got sick of it so I started feeding the flowers to the livestock.

"My women come when I call and leave when the tilling is over," said Cúchulainn. "As it should be."

I had to smile. *Funny little rooster of a guy*, that Cúchulainn. Always making a spectacle of himself. If he lived in the twenty-first century he'd be driving an MG convertible with his comb-over flapping in the breeze and a skinny, bleached-blond trophy wife in the passenger seat. It made me wonder how Stuart and Carrie's honeymoon was going.

"She may have a point, you know," I said. "It takes time to find out what someone is really like."

He looked puzzled. "What do you mean? People are what they are. A person of honor hides nothing," he declared.

I was tempted to explain to him about psychology and stuff, but why bother? Freud hadn't even been born yet. "Maybe so," I said. "But how do you know if someone is a person of honor?"

"If you have to ask"—he shrugged—"that's your answer. Slay them before they slay you."

I should remember that advice, I thought. *It could come in handy for junior year.*

Fergus burst back into the cottage, his face flushed. This time he was carrying an entire shrub. It looked like an azalea in full bloom, yanked whole from the ground. The dirt was still clinging to its roots.

"Oh!" I said in dismay. "That's enough flowers for now, Fergus. Let's see if we can replant that one. It would look very nice by the front door."

Fergus dropped the shrub. "There is some commotion by the castle!" he announced. "The jewelry maker is threatening to leave! She says she will never come back!"

Cúchulainn's eyes turned into two blinking red turn signals. "Says she!" he growled, heading for the door. "I'll bring her back, never fear." A dust cloud started to whirl in a tiny spiral above his head.

"Guys!" I shouted, as I jumped up and body blocked the door. The goat spied the pile of flowers that fell out of my lap and started munching. "Relax! She has to be *willing*. That's the whole point. Calm down. Give her some space."

"You talk to her, Morganne," Fergus begged. "You found Erin, and you found the woman of fire and gold. Surely only you can help this woman find her own will to marry King Conor."

I suspected he was right, but I also suspected that the jewelry woman and I could not resolve this alone. "I'll talk to them both," I said.

"Don't trouble the king about this matter," said Cúchulainn.

"I have to," I said. "It takes two to tango."

The word *tango* echoed in my head. I had a sudden feeling that I'd stumbled on to something, but what was it?

"To what?" asked Fergus.

"To dance," I said, holding my arms out to him. Fergus joyfully hurdled over the goat to embrace me, and I let him nibble on my neck while I tried to figure out what I might say to the king and this woman to help true love blossom.

"i hate to say this, but he really is a pig. have you ever seen him eat?"

"It's not my fault!" cried the king. "I'm under a spell!"

"Right. And I'm Queen of the Faeries."

This was not going well.

I racked my brains. Other than my months with Raph, I didn't have much relationship experience to bring to bear as a couples' counselor. My parents got along pretty well, I guess, but I'd never thought about why. They were Mom and Dad, they were together, I took it for granted. Which I shouldn't have, since half the kids at school had parents who were either divorced or so cold and mean to each other that their children wished they were.

By the time I'd arrived at the castle, someone had finally bothered to find out that the jewelry woman's name was Dana. Now the three of us were sequestered in the king's royal chambers, with the usual gang of armed warrior-dudes standing guard at the door.

Dana gestured to them. "You see what it's like here? How could a person live like this? It's so tense!"

Conor pounded his fist. "I'm a king! I have responsibilities! You want me to walk away from all that? Who's going to pay the bills?"

Dana crossed her arms. "I may not own a castle, but I have

a thriving business, remember? I've been paying my own way for quite some time, and if you think that just because you were born a king you can boss me around, you are talking to the wrong woman."

Conor turned to me and threw his hands up. "You see? She's impossible. Are you sure she's the right one?"

"Hear that? He's not even interested in me!" She was just as mad. "He only cares about this stupid spell. Once it's broken, who knows what will happen to me?"

"You make me sound like an ogre," the king grumbled.

"Don't talk to me about ogres," she snapped. "I've dated ogres, and it was damned exciting, I have to tell you." She leaned back on the tufted cushions. "That doesn't mean I'd marry one."

There was something about the way these two argued. Like they'd been together for years and years. Instant chemistry, but they'd really gotten off on the wrong foot, what with her being kidnapped and him being under a spell and all.

We argued like an old married couple the moment we met. That's how Lucia described her first meeting with Jack Faraday. Could these two be soul mates as well? Maybe, but how could I get them to stop arguing and realize that for themselves?

"Do either of you guys know how to tango?" I said, impulsively. Since the tango had not been invented yet, I was pretty sure the answer would be no.

"No," they said in unison. It was the first thing they'd agreed on.

"Good," I said. "I'll teach you."

* * *

Why the tango? It was the only two-person dance I knew, and I only knew it because Sarah was the dance lead in the school production of the musical *The Pajama Game* freshman year and she had to do the big tango number. She'd taught me the guy's part so she could practice. We'd had some hilarious good times dancing around and knocking stuff over in her living room, believe me.

But now I was going for romance, not comedy. I needed King Conor and Dana to hold hands and put their arms around each other's waists and shut up long enough to feel the chemistry that was lurking underneath the surface. The tango would be the magic love spell this strawberry-blond goddess was about to cast over the sparring, star-crossed couple, and I really hoped it worked because I didn't know what else to do.

One rather silly-sounding worry crossed my mind as I coaxed my two dancing students into position: Was there any chance that introducing the tango to ancient Irish culture at this point in time would change the course of history? Prime Directive purists would say, *You betcha*, but come on—it was just a little dance.

The only tango music I knew was "Hernando's Hideaway" from *The Pajama Game,* as plunked out on an out-of-tune piano on Sarah's rehearsal tape. I couldn't remember any of the words, so we had to settle for me singing and clapping, "Bum, de bum, de bum bum bum!"

I taught them the steps I could remember and made up the rest, and over the course of the afternoon I managed to get King Conor and Dana doing a very basic, half-remembered version of a high-school musical version of a Broadway show version of the tango. Authentic? Hell no, but that wasn't my goal.

"Whoops! I stepped on your foot!" Dana laughed.

"My fault, my fault," said King Conor. "I think I'm a few beats behind. Are my hands too sweaty?"

"Not at all," Dana replied. "Shall we take it from the top?"

"That's enough for today!" I said, wiping my brow with my flowy cream-colored sleeve, which was now tinged a mossy shade of green from my several under-sea and under-swamp excursions. "Tomorrow we'll add the spins. And we definitely need some real music."

"Do you mind if we practice more after you go?" asked King Conor. "If, of course, Dana is willing."

"I would be delighted," she said. They turned back to each other. It was like they'd forgotten I was even in the room.

Tammy was swimming—no, it was Sophie Billingsley, at least it looked like Sophie but I knew it was really Tammy somehow—anyway, she was swimming underwater and I was with her and we weren't mermaids at all, we were us and we needed to breathe *now*, and we swam and kicked but it seemed like we weren't getting any closer to the surface—

"Wake up," crooned a male voice.

"Colin," I mumbled. "I was dreaming."

"It's Fergus, beloved."

I breathed in the strong, familiar smell of earth and grass and horses, and I opened my eyes. It was Fergus smiling at me. Then I remembered. After I'd picked the right moment to give King Conor and Dana some privacy, Fergus and I had decided to take Sam out for a graze. I must have fallen asleep in the grass.

"Dreaming of your other world, eh?" Fergus said.

My first impulse was to shrug off the question, but a person of honor hides nothing, after all. "My sister," I said. "Her name is Tammy."

Fergus started massaging my tired dancing feet, a task he performed as if it made him the happiest man in the world. "A sister! Is she magic like you?"

"She's interested in magic, that's for sure. Magic kingdoms, especially." I smiled, thinking of Tammy's Disney addiction, and how she'd sit there singing in front of the TV. "And she says she can see faeries in the garden."

"Well, ye'd have to be blind not to see faeries in the garden." Fergus laughed. "They're common as weeds! But I'm glad her eyes are healthy. And this 'Colin'—your brother, I suppose?"

I wondered if maybe he was fishing for boyfriend dirt, but Fergus was not the type to fish. "No," I said. "He's a friend. But the two of you could be brothers, you're very alike."

"Poor fellow!" Fergus said. "If he's very like me, he must be in love with you. And if we met, we'd have no end of fighting! Better if we didn't."

Of course they would never meet, I thought. But would I ever see Colin again? Or was Long-ago my world, now? It had been a night and a day since I popped up in the swamp with Erin, the longest time I'd spent here.

"Fergus," I asked, leaning back in the grassy meadow. "Could you explain something to me?"

He smiled and moved his attention to my calves. "Anything, beloved."

"Everyone keeps saying I've got faery blood or I'm part goddess." Sam gave a little nicker from where he was munching nearby.

"Not part," Sam said, his mouth full. "Half."

Even a horse knew more about me than I did. "I can't remember anything about it," I said. "Who are my parents?"

Fergus's fingers were digging into my calf muscles with just the right amount of pressure. "If I tell you, will you let me kiss you?"

"You can kiss me anyway!" I laughed. "But tell me first."

"You are Morganne," Fergus said softly. "You're the daughter of a mortal man and faery queen. Your father was lured into the vale of the Immortal Ones by a powerful enchantress."

"A faery queen? Are you sure?" I thought of my real mother, my Connecticut mother, the coupon-clipping queen of Lucky Lou's.

"Aye. There she seduced him and together they tilled the fields of passion until a child was conceived. Afterward your father awoke in the tender grass with naught but the clothes on his back and sweet, sweet memories."

Sam gave an appreciative snort, but it might have been more about the tender grass than the miracle of my conception.

"Nine months later he was summoned by a crow that spoke to him in the language of birds," Fergus went on. "The crow led him back to the faery mound, where a babe in arms was given to him to raise." He smiled, as if I should know the rest.

A faery mound. "I think I know the place," I said. "Was the baby me?"

"'Twas you yourself, Morganne. Half human, half divine. And with you came a prophecy."

Duh. Did anything come without a prophecy in these parts?

"What was it?" I was almost afraid to know.

"That though Morganne would not live among us, she was one of us, to love and to long for but never possess." He smiled a sad smile. "And whenever the people of King Conor's realm needed a champion to intercede with the Lordly Ones, Morganne would appear and offer her help. But she would never stay past the time of her service."

"And my father?"

Sam stamped his feet.

"Killed in battle long ago," said Fergus gently.

I didn't know how to feel about that. "Thank you for telling me," I said.

Fergus took my hands in his. "May I take my payment?"

Like I would say no. Sam was kind enough to look away, and Fergus laid a smooch on me that promised to leave scorch marks on the earth.

"Morganne," he whispered. "Are you sure? I know you told me we are forbidden to consummate our love—"

I put my finger to his lips. "You heard the prophecy," I said. "It's just not a good idea."

"This See Vee Ess must be a very powerful wizard, then." He took my face in his hands and ran his fingers through my long, thick, shampoo-commercial hair. "I'd eat you up like a bowl of gruel if I could," he murmured, before kissing me again.

"What?" My voice was muffled by the kiss.

"I said, I'd eat you up like a bowl . . ."

But I'd heard what he said.

poor colin. When i swam off with the merrow at the beach, where could he possibly think I'd gone? If I disappeared under the water and never came back, he'd have swum the ocean himself trying to find me.

What a good guy, I thought. *What a nice, funny, decent, ordinary, great kisser of a guy.*

It was sort of tacky to be thinking of Colin while kissing Fergus, but sort of not. They were so alike, after all: both trustworthy warrior-dudes in their respective Irish, hunky, cornflower-blue-eyed ways.

I hope he's okay. I hope he didn't drown trying to rescue me or get fired for losing one of the customers or, oh fek, get arrested for murder. That would really suck.

"Why so sad, my love?" whispered Fergus.

"It's hard to explain," I said. "Homesick, I guess."

"I wish I could see your home," he murmured. "Connecticut, you call it? I wish you could take me there."

I couldn't help smiling at the thought. "That would be awesome," I said.

"Totally," he agreed.

* * *

later, after a sweet smooch session with Fergus and a pleasant ride back to the dun on Sam's back, I sat in front of the fire, mulling and thinking about all Fergus had told me. It was quiet, and the dancing flames seemed able to light up corners of my brain that had been sitting in the shadows for a long time. Only then did I understand the full meaning of the prophecy about baby me, the semigoddess Morganne.

And whenever the people of King Conor's realm needed a champion to intercede with the Lordly Ones, Morganne would appear and offer her help. But she would never stay past the time of her service. . . .

I was in Long-ago to break these enchantments. Once I did that, I'd be outta here. Back to my own time, though exactly when and where I'd land I had no clue.

And if I didn't? If I couldn't figure out how to break the spells, or if I tried and failed, or if I just gave up and sat around playing with my hair and sulking?

Then I'd stay Morganne, happily ever after in the Magic Kingdom of Long-ago Land, decked out in a long Disney princess dress with a hunky warrior-dude boyfriend and no reliable form of contraceptives.

What I understood is that I had a choice. I could get the job done and go home, or I could relax. Go with the flow. Stay.

Stay? In Long-ago? And miss the junior prom? No thanks. The hair was fun, but so what. I could always let mine grow out.

I knew what I needed to do.

* * *

i needed to hire a band.

For the tangoing twosome to make it all the way to the altar (or the shrine or the sacred grotto or wherever it was the Druids performed their ceremonies), they would need more than me bum-bumming my way through "Hernando's Hideaway." They would need ambience, the kind only live music can provide. Call it YBCSWB: Your Basic Castle Scene With Band.

But how would I find a band? It's not like I could just log onto MySpace and click on MP3s until I found one I liked.

Fergus was too busy carving our names in the sides of trees to be of practical assistance. Much as I hated to stroke his ego, I asked Cúchulainn for advice.

"Dude," I said. "We need a band. Where can I find some musicians?"

Cúchulainn stopped polishing his armor long enough to heap some friendly scorn upon me. "Morganne, for a semidivinity, you are an inexplicably ignorant woman," he said. "This is Ireland. Everyone is a musician."

"Great," I said. "Send some over to the king's hall. Rehearsal's at three. I'll be teaching them a show tune."

by the time the second royal dancing lesson was convened, King Conor and Queen-in-training Dana were holding hands even when they weren't practicing the tango.

"Hernando's Hideaway" sounded a little odd played on the harp and the drum and the wooden flute, but the beat was solid and the royal couple-to-be had the steps down. We added some simple turns and I felt the time was right to do my goddess-of-love thing and give King Conor and Dana a nudge.

"You two look great together," I commented. "If you don't mind me asking, have you had a chance to talk any more about, you know—the relationship?"

They both got a bit bashful. King Conor started picking threads out of his royal robes.

"Guys!" I scolded. "A good relationship is all about communication." This I knew from my mom's subscription to *O, The Oprah Magazine*. My mom is very big on Dr. Phil. "Talk!"

Now they both started laughing. "All is well, Morganne," said King Conor. "The truth is—in a way—we have already wed."

Whoa! Was this what life was like before the tabloids? A king could get married and nobody knew? I was shocked.

"Conor, that is so sweet!" said Dana, looking deeply into his eyes. "But you'd best tell her what happened." She looked very pleased with herself. "It might affect the enchantment."

The king cleared his throat. "After we were done with our dancing we took a walk in the moonlight, and, well, one thing led to another."

"And?" I said, crossing my arms. I sounded exactly like my parents did when they were pumping me for information about where I'd been, what I'd done and who I'd done it with.

"Well, he's a great kisser," explained Dana.

"And, well. One thing led to another," repeated the king. The two of them giggled.

Well well well. Sounded like some royal tilling had occurred.

"Congratulations, you two!" I said, but I knew it wasn't enough. *Wed fire and gold to the king.* Tilling was all very well, but to break the enchantment they were going to have to take it to the next level. "I'm very happy for you. But don't you think we should celebrate a little? Make it, you know, official?"

"Not a feast!" moaned Conor. "If we have a wedding feast before this curse is lifted, I'll just end up eating myself silly." He looked at Dana. "That wouldn't be very romantic."

"But won't getting married break the spell?" asked Dana, sounding alarmed. "You promised me once we were married you'd change. No more uncontrollable eating and drinking, remember?"

"Um. Um. Um," King Conor stammered.

"Because I *really* like to entertain!" she went on. "And I don't want to find out after it's too late that you cannot behave like a gentleman at a dinner party!"

"Um. Um." He looked at me for help.

"The spell *will* be broken, I promise! But there's one more part of the enchantment I have to solve." I looked over at the musicians and gave them the get-ready nod. "It's really easy: We just have to win a war without killing anyone." *Not that I have any clue how to do that,* I thought, leading King Conor and Dana to our improvised dance floor. "I'm working on it. In the meantime, how about a celebration that's not all about food? A simple exchange of vows, perhaps?"

Dana took a deep breath and looked at King Conor. She really liked him; it was all over her face. "I could make us some lovely rings," she suggested.

"And then—a dance?" King Conor smiled shyly at his already-bedded, soon-to-be-wedded bride-to-be. I cued the band with a nod.

"A dance!" She smiled and stretched out one arm, striking a very nice tango pose. "That would be perfect."

eighteen

What's lost in the earth must be found,
But the earth must be turned without tilling.

Check.

Wed fire and gold to the king,
But the lady herself must be willing.

Check check.

Let rivals come forth to do battle,
But the war must be won without killing.

Let rivals come forth to do battle. I didn't like the sound of that one bit. For one thing, it sounded serious, like if we didn't get it right people *would* get killed. That might be all in a day's slaying to Cúchulainn and Fergus, but still—it made me anxious. I didn't even like to smoosh bugs.

There was something else bothering me too: The keys to solving the first two enchantments had been provided by my other, actual, Morgan self. Only after my date with Colin (where we moved the earth without tilling, sigh!) did the merrow appear and lead me to Erin. And only after I found the lost gold earring of the fiery-tempered Carrie Pippin was I able to peek back into Long-ago and recognize the woman of "fire and gold" the king was meant to marry.

But now that a couple of days in Long-ago time had passed, it didn't feel like I was going back to my bike tour anytime soon. Would I ever? Had I disappeared altogether from my own century, or was Morgan-me living out a whole life in some other time-space continuum (thank you, *Star Trek*) that I didn't know about, while Morganne-me was spending her summer vacation in King Conorville giving dance class and lamely attempting to undo enchantments?

If so, I hoped the other me was having fun. If I never made it back, I hoped she would have a nice summer and find a nice boyfriend next year, nicer than Raph for sure, and maybe get back into playing field hockey, and get her driver's license and go to the prom whether she had a date or not, and spend more time with Sarah and the rest of her old friends before graduation and get into a decent college and pick some sort of interesting career and have a pleasant life.

As for Morganne, the semidivinity—I might have to figure this one out without any help from Morgan, the cranky suburban teen. The irony did not escape me.

Let rivals come forth to do battle. Clearly all hell was about to break loose. But until it did, we would dance the tango at a royal wedding.

i was expecting the druid priest to be like gandalf from the *Lord of the Rings* movies, but she was actually a priest*ess*, and a young one at that. She was tall and fair and sporty looking and babbled her incantations in a strange, guttural Druid dialect. She reminded me of Heidi, in fact. Poor Heidi. If I ever saw her again I would offer to take a nice picture of her.

The ceremony was short and sweet, with the high point being the exchange of the rings. Dana had made a matching pair of her own design—each one a beautiful gold band that ended in a pair of hands holding a single heart between them.

Afterward, while all the loyal subjects of King Conor's realm (who'd been warned to eat beforehand, since no food would be served) were gamely imitating the royal couple and inventing their own strange and wonderful versions of the tango, Fergus and I went over to compliment Dana on her jewelry design.

The newlyweds held out their hands so we could see the rings up close. The two-hands-clasped pattern looked strangely familiar to me.

"I think it would be nicer with a crown on top," teased King Conor.

"No, no, a crown is too much. It's vulgar!" Dana said. For a minute I was afraid we were about to witness their first official marital spat. But then Dana took his hand.

"But of course, my husband, if you want one, I can always add a crown."

That's when I started to cry.

"Beautiful, isn't it?" Fergus was misty-eyed too.

"Yes, but it's just—" I knew he couldn't really understand, but I'd just figured it out and my heart was so full I had to share the moment with someone. "There was this episode of *Buffy*, when she and Angel are about to say good-bye, and he gives her a ring exactly like that, because it's an old Irish tradition, and now, look—it's all starting right here, and here we are, how cool is that?"

"Buffy?" said Fergus. "Who's Buffy?"

"Grab your weapons! the castle is under attack!"

Typical. Even at the king's wedding, Cúchulainn found a way to be the center of attention. Galloping into the middle of the dance on Samhain's back, hollering and waving his sword-thingy around and working all his hero special effects like it was sweeps week. Right when Fergus and I were in the middle of a nice tango dip too.

"NO WEAPONS!" I yelled. "Cúchulainn, put that tornado away right now! There is to be *no fighting*." God, I sounded like my mom.

"But an invading army is at the castle gates! They want to steal our cattle and our women! They are *pissing me off*!" roared Cúchulainn. Poor Sam was dropping big fragrant horse turds on the dance floor, out of excitement, I guess.

There would be no rest for the weary enchantment-breaking semigoddess, obviously. "'The war must be won without killing,' remember?" I said, swatting away the sparks that were flying off Cúchulainn's forehead and threatening to set my dress on fire. "Do you want to get rid of these enchantments or not?"

He pouted, and his tornado downgraded itself to a couple of smoke rings. "Fine. I won't slaughter them all single-handedly and mount their bloody severed heads on the parapets, though naturally I *could*." He sounded miffed and petulantly turned to his king. "No killing! Feh. What would you like me to do *instead*?"

King Conor looked at his new queen, and then back to Cúchulainn. "We should invite them in, I suppose," the king said, patting Dana's hand. "I hope they've already eaten. Who is their commander?"

Even Cúchulainn looked a bit worried. "Queen Maeve," he said.

Porn-star Maeve? Complete with her own army? How hot is *that*?

Who is more fierce and fine than Queen Maeve?

Nobody. This woman was buffer, cooler and I do mean *endowed* with more action-hero sex appeal than all three of Charlie's Angels put together. She galloped up to the castle on a chestnut stallion like she was roaring into town on a Harley-Davidson.

"Who do I kill first?" she bellowed, as her horse reared up and threw a few taunting punches with its hooves. "And where do you keep the *real* men?" Wisely, King Conor had sent his more unflappable advisers to greet her; otherwise the fight would have been on before the warrior-queen dismounted.

After some heated negotiations, Maeve agreed to postpone the lopping-off-limbs action and "parley." As far as I could tell, both sides took this to mean that they would sit down and chat for a while before taking it outside to hack each other to bits.

I knew a thing or two about randy Queen Maeve and what rocked her world, thanks to Colin's lunchtime mythology lesson (thirty guys a day or Super-Tilling with the Mythic Stud Fergus, in case you've forgotten). But what I didn't know was whether *my* Fergus was *her* Fergus, and if he was, whether their uh, relationship, had already happened or was in the future. Easy enough to find out, though.

"That Maeve, she's really something, isn't she?" Through the ramparts of the castle Fergus and I watched her leap off her horse and hand the reins to one of her warriors.

"Who?" he murmured. He was standing close behind me, dreamily inhaling the scent of my hair.

"Queen Maeve," I said. Now she was squatting in the dirt to pee. Nice of her to take care of that before going indoors. "Have you two ever met?"

"In battle? No, I've not yet had the privilege of clashing swords with the warrior queen." His breath was warm on my neck. "Though that may change before the day is out."

Warrior-dudes! Fighting and tilling, it was all they ever thought about. "No, Fergus," I said. "I meant *socially*."

He shrugged, as if I'd named a weapon he'd never heard of. "No, not that way either."

"She's awfully pretty," I said. "Don't you think?"

Fergus laughed. "Morganne, there is no other woman in the world, pretty or otherwise. Only you."

What a cutie he was. But as entertaining as I found Fergus's devotion, I knew it wasn't under his control, which sort of took the fun out of it. I also knew that if I was lucky, maybe not today, maybe not tomorrow, but soon and for who knows how long, I'd be disappearing again, and that was something *I* couldn't control.

During all my months with Raph it was understood—at the time of his choosing, I'd be the one to get dumped. The thought that I could have broken up with *him* was so outside Raph's reality that somehow it never occurred to me either.

With Fergus, I would be the one to leave. We both knew it. I cared about him and I honestly didn't want him to get hurt. But cookies crumble, sometimes. What could I say?

It was great going out with you. We had some fun, right? You'll have a great summer, Fergus. You'll meet randy warrior queens and, whatever.

Score points for Raph, I guess. Maybe he'd been trying to be nice, in his own self-involved way.

I watched Queen Maeve sashay into the castle. No matter what happened between us, Fergus would, in time, get over it. Of that I was sure. The evidence was sashaying before my eyes, and it had some serious queenly junk in the trunk.

"That's very sweet, Fergus," I said gently. "But it's possible that you might feel otherwise, after the full moon comes."

"It is possible," he said, holding me closer, "that I might not."

*   *   *

"'the war must be won without *killing*?' that's the most fekked-up thing I've ever heard!" Maeve had demanded mead be served all around, and she and her inner circle of bodyguards were swilling away inside the royal parley chamber. I hoped this didn't count as a feast. If it did, King Conor would be in a mead stupor till morning, and there goes the wedding night. So far he seemed able to resist, though, and Dana was keeping a watchful eye on him.

"There are only two ways to decide a battle," said Queen Maeve, after releasing a hearty belch. "All-out war or single combat."

"On this we agree," said Cúchulainn. "Let's choose our champions and meet on the battlefield. I nominate—me!"

"And I accept your challenge!" hollered Maeve, her spit flying into his face.

"Guys," I interrupted. "Calm down. Single combat is, like, violent. Someone could get hurt."

Queen Maeve, Cúchulainn, King Conor, Dana and their respective warrior-dude flunkies all looked at me like, *Duh, isn't that the point?* To think that a society could be this blood-thirsty, and video games had not even been invented yet.

"Now I realize mass slaughter is all in a day's work for you," I went on, "but we have specific instructions here. No killing."

"And why? So *your people* will be rid of the terrible enchantments! What's in it for *me*?" Maeve slammed her empty mead cup down on the table and someone promptly refilled it. She narrowed her eyes. "Why should I go along with this ridiculousness?"

"A, nobody gets killed," I offered. Queen Maeve laughed,

and all her warriors laughed along with her in a rather ass-kissy way, if I may say so.

"B, do *you* want to piss off the Lordly Ones?" I could see I needed to get tough with this crowd, so I copied Maeve's narrow-eyed expression, which was very intimidating and Clint Eastwood–like. "How would you like it if the faery folk decided to pick on *your* neighborhood next?"

Maeve narrowed her eyes even further, into mean-queen slits. "Is that a threat? Is that what *your people* plan?"

"I'm just saying," I said, bluffing my ass off. "Play ball with me or suffer the consequences."

Play ball with me. Is that what I'd just said? My voice started to echo weirdly in my skull. By the time my head cleared I realized King Conor was talking to me. "Tell us, wise Morganne! Among your people, when two tribes are at war, how is the victor decided, unless it be by the death of one or the other?"

"We have many death-free ways to decide things." Even I could hear how wimpy that sounded, so I started shouting in an attempt to appear more goddess-leader-of-tomorrow-like. "Eeny meeny miney mo, for example!" I yelled. "We flip coins! We make cootie catchers!"

"Cootie catchers!" someone murmured, impressed.

"When my dad needs help deciding something, he calls his lawyer or his accountant," I bellowed. "When my mom needs help, she asks her therapist!" My listeners were hanging on my every word. "And both of them frequently consult *Consumer Reports*."

"But who would you yourself consult?" demanded Cúchulainn.

"The wisest ones of all." I thought of my stacks of college brochures, and my voice grew ominous-sounding. "They are called Guidance Counselors."

The king looked glum. "Would that we had so many helpful wizards among us! But I fear we are beyond the sage advice of your lawyers and therapists and guidance counselors. The people demand all-out war between two rival kingdoms, and the people's will must be satisfied."

Rival kingdoms? I thought hard. *Rival kingdoms* . . .

East Norwich High School's biggest rival was Old Southport. This had been going on for years. Kids at school whose parents had graduated from East Norwich were still carrying grudges from lost football games of thirty years prior. Parking lot shouting matches between East Norwich dads and Old Southport dads were not unheard of.

Play ball with me. "When my people want to prevail over our rivals," I said, my head spinning with the beauty and rightness of what I was about to say, "we play football. That is what we do. And that is what you must do as well."

"Very well," the king said. "Teach us how."

Great. I knew jack shit about football, but then again King Conor and Queen Maeve and all their minions had never heard of the NFL, so who cared? I told them all I could remember, which was basically two teams running back and forth, trying to get a ball through goalposts. There was kicking and running and throwing involved. The more I described, the bigger their eyes grew, and soon they were muttering and pounding the butt ends of their spears on the ground.

"Hurling!" someone cried finally. "She wants the battle decided by a hurling match!"

"Woot! Woot!" Everyone, including Cúchulainn, seemed jazzed by this idea.

"Gross!" I cried. A farting contest was one thing, but hurling? That was beyond frat boy.

"Hurling! Hurling!" The chant went up and the spears pounded, until I thought I might throw up myself.

nineteen

do not get sick, here. As it turns out, hurling back then is not what hurling is now.

It's an actual sport. There are two teams and a field with goalposts on either end. Each player carries a stick called a hurley, and there's a little ball made of leather that you have to whack through the goalposts.

Fergus and Cúchulainn and Queen Maeve and everyone else in the parley chamber were shouting over each other trying to explain all this to me, when an unexpected visitor appeared in our midst.

When I say appeared, I mean *appeared*, like shifting shadows that suddenly form into a shape you glimpse out of the corner of your eye. A breath later he shimmered fully into being. Fergus and I noticed him first, but that was probably because we'd met him before.

It was the boy, the faery boy we'd seen by the swamp. The one who had taken Erin.

For a moment I was afraid Fergus would throttle him, but before anyone could move the boy smiled and spoke.

"Hello, Morgan. Nice of you to come back."

Swift as pulling out a plug, the wild sports-bar din in the parley chamber turned to silence.

"Why do you call me Morgan?" I asked cautiously.

"Dumb question!" The boy guffawed. "It's your name, isn't it?"

In another time-space continuum it *was* my name, or would be—but that was too much to try to explain right now, especially since I was the only person in the room who'd ever seen an episode of *Star Trek*. "Yes," I said. "I suppose it is."

"Just because *I* am a dreadful speller, *she* thinks she is two different people!" he said, to the open-mouthed crowd. "'Tis a silly girl who doesn't know who she is!" The boy laughed. "But you've always been a silly girl."

"Do we know each other?" I asked. I sensed I was in delicate territory here. "If we do, I'm sorry, I don't remember. Please tell me."

He made the saddest face, as if he might cry. "I know you don't remember, and it's awful!" he whined. "To not even be remembered by my own sister!"

Everyone gasped. I tried to play it cool. "I don't remember very much about the Land of Faery," I said gently, the way people talk when they're coaxing suicidal strangers off the edges of bridges. "It's nothing personal. Perhaps I'm under some sort of spell."

"Or perhaps you just don't love me anymore!" He seemed genuinely upset. "But very well, I will play your forgetting game. When you were a child there were days we danced among the foxgloves and painted the flowers all their bright colors. We climbed the lilies of the valley like ladders and sipped the nectar of hollyhocks until we were giddy with the sweetness." He bit his lip. "And you don't remember me at all, do you?"

The look on my face must have given me away.

"I'm Finnbar," he pleaded. "I'm your brother. Remember? We swore it that day on the swings, the ones that squeaked and groaned?"

We had a swing set in the yard when I was little, I remembered. *At our old house, the one we lived in before Tammy was born, the one that had rooms and doors . . .*

All at once he was happy again. "No matter." He giggled. "Because now we will get to play together. I do love to play at hurleys! Morgan, you will be captain of your team."

"Unfair!" cried Queen Maeve, turning to King Conor. "You will have *her*—one of the Faery Folk—on your team. She will use her magic to cheat." She glared at me.

"But I don't—"

"It's an unfair advantage," Maeve declared.

"But I don't even—"

"True," mused Finnbar, ignoring my protest. "But never fear, Queen Maeve. I will play on *your* team. That will even things up."

"But I don't even know how to play hurling," I cried.

"Don't worry, dear sister. It's very simple," Finnbar said, with a mischievous smile. "It's a lot like field hockey."

* * *

"So you can throw the ball but not kick it?" the rules of hurling had me totally confused, and I only had an hour to learn them.

"No!" cried Fergus and Cúchulainn simultaneously. "You can catch it but not throw it—"

"You can hit it with the hurley stick—"

"You can carry it on the hurley—"

"You can bounce it on the hurley—"

"You can kick it when it's on the ground, and you can catch it when it's in the air—"

"—but you must *never* pick it up when it's on the ground!"

"That's a foul."

"Very foul."

The two of them looked at me as if this were all self-evident. Erin had just finished painting blue war paint on their faces, and now she was doing mine. It tickled and I wanted to rub my nose.

"Hold still, Captain!" she said, brushing a blue curlicue around my eye. "Else how will we tell the teams apart?"

I wiggled my nose to stop the itch but it didn't help. Of all the strange adventures Long-ago had offered me so far, somehow, being plunged into the universal gym-class nightmare was the worst. *It's gym class. You're captain of your team. The game begins, but you can't remember the rules. Everyone is looking at you, waiting for you to do something. . . .*

"And what is the point of the game, exactly?"

"It's easy, Morganne! You simply have to get the sliothar

through the goal." Fergus was looking totally buff and *Braveheart*-like, painted and shirtless and holding his hurley stick like Fred Flintstone's club. If I wasn't so freaked out by having to learn this game I would have been very distracted.

"Sorry," I said, turning my head so Erin could do the other side. "But what's the sliothar again?"

Fergus sighed. "The ball, Morganne. Keep your eye on the sliothar and everything will be all right."

Cúchulainn, it turned out, was a fanatical hurley player.

"Have you never heard that story?" he asked, incredulous. "That's how I got the name Cúchulainn. It was years ago, when I was just a boy—"

"Not now, okay?" We were walking to the field and I was not in a good mood. It would be impossible to play hurling in a long flowy princess dress, but gym suits had yet to be invented, so I was wearing some leather pants of Fergus's that were too big for me, belted around my waist with a rope, and a rough cotton shirt.

Needless to say, the sports bra had not been invented yet either. There was chafing and bouncing going on, and I did not like it one bit.

"It's an essential part of my legend—but as you wish," said Cúchulainn, sounding disappointed. Fergus had gone ahead to gather flowers to give me in case we won. Very optimistic, in my opinion.

"Let's review," said Cúchulainn. "If you get the sliothar

through the top of the goal, it's one point, through the bottom is three."

"Shut up," I said. "I can't remember any more."

"You can run with the sliothar in your hand, four steps only. Five steps is a foul."

"Shut up," I muttered, walking faster.

"After four steps you can bounce it on the hurley and back to your hand, but you can only do that twice."

"Shut *up*, okay?"

I saw his eyes get that red-eye look people have in bad photos. "Morganne, how do you expect us to win if our captain doesn't even know the rules?"

"Cúchulainn, we *will* win, because we *have* to win!" I yelled, sounding very unhinged and uncaptainlike. "But we have to win without anyone getting killed! And if you don't stop hammering me about the fekkin' rules I'm going to beat you to death right now with this hurley stick! Got it?"

For the first time, Cúchulainn looked at me with real respect. "Aye, Captain!"

He sounded just like Scotty in *Star Trek*.

A pristine new hurling field had magically appeared in Samhain's favorite grazing meadow. This didn't really come as a surprise. By now I understood that Faery Folk, even spoiled little boy Faery Folk, could do some major magic.

What did surprise me was that the field was surrounded by an enormous open-air stadium, with rings of bleachers rising all around. And the stadium was packed.

Thousands upon thousands of spectators were waiting for the game to begin, excited and laughing and unpacking their picnic baskets. I'd been to see the Yankees play at Yankee Stadium a few times with my dad, and the size of this crowd was definitely in that ballpark, if you will excuse the expression. Main difference being, these spectators were *special*.

They were the Faery Folk. Many of them were tall and beautiful, with the lithe grace Finnbar had. These faeries were dressed in elegant clothes from every conceivable era, like a reference book on costume design come to life. But there were other types of magical beings too: short troll-like creatures, tiny flower-faeries that flitted about nervously, a crowd of massive hairy ogres getting into a fight near a hot-dog vendor. There was even a splash-zone section down front that was reserved for merrows, all of whom carried big sport bottles filled with water and were helpfully squirting each other to keep cool.

The more I scanned the crowd, the more odd things I noticed: Tinker Bell from the Disney version of *Peter Pan*. The kids from my middle-school production of *A Midsummer Night's Dream*, still in costume. A garden gnome my dad bought at a garage sale and put on the front lawn as a joke last summer (at the moment the gnome was slathering himself with sunblock). The animatronic vegetables and farm animals from Lucky Lou's, the excitable blond guy from *Queer Eye* — I saw all of them in the stands, alive and chatty and happily anticipating the game that was soon to begin.

Too. Much. Information. If I let myself get addled by what I was seeing, my razor-thin grasp of hurling would be knocked right out of my head, so I forced myself to turn away and walk onto the field. As I did, I caught a glimpse of another creature—a very short little man, dressed in green and waving at me from between the legs of a tall faery woman in a beaded flapper dress—

"Fergus!" I grabbed his arm. "Look! Do you see that?"

"See what, Captain?"

"I could have sworn I—See! He's right there, watching us from behind his pot of gold—"

"Calm down, darling," said Fergus. From the pumped-up way he twirled his hurley stick I could tell he was eager for the game to begin. "Now you're imagining things."

"But don't you see him?" I was amazed. "In that three-cornered hat, he's no taller than my knee—look, he's smoking a pipe! He's winking at us!"

"You're just nervous, my love. Believing the tales we tell children at bedtime." He tugged my arm gently to lead me out to the field. Whatever I'd seen was gone.

"But the faeries"—I looked around at the packed stadium, worried that I'd lost my mind relative even to Long-ago standards—"you can see them, right? You believe they're real?"

He looked at me with fond indulgence. "That's because faeries *are* real, Morganne! But there's no such thing as leprechauns. Everyone knows that!"

He kissed me quickly and took his place at the goal.

twenty

the faeries had left one small, noticeably ram-
shackle section of bleachers roped off and marked with a mis-
spelled sign: HEWMANS SIT HEARE. Erin was seated with the
humans, of course, as were King Conor and the newly
queened Dana.

I waved at Erin, and she waved back. I hoped it didn't
make her nervous sitting so close to all those faery folk after
what happened to her at the swamp, but she seemed fine,
bouncy and revved-up about the game.

Cúchulainn and I were front-line offense, with a row of
three defensive players behind us, chosen from among King
Conor's buffest warrior-dudes. As we lined up in our posi-
tions I wondered what was about to happen. Once the game
was over and (hopefully) the enchantments were broken,
would I be whisked away again to my bike tour, to Connecticut, to parts unknown? I should have said good-bye to Fergus,

just in case, but he was playing goalie and the game was about to begin.

Finnbar and Maeve were the front offensive line for their team. That meant they were standing directly in front of us. Finnbar was dressed in a spotless Victorian fencing outfit, complete with face mask.

"I hope you enjoy the game," he shouted through the mask. "It was so much trouble to arrange!"

"This stadium couldn't have been that difficult for you to whip up," I said.

"Not the stadium, you ding-dong! I mean putting all those enchantments everywhere until you came back! And then waiting *forever* while you figured out my clues!"

Could I possibly be dumb enough to have not figured this out already? "Wait," I said. "Did *you* put all the enchantments on King Conor's people?"

Finnbar giggled and did a little soft-shoe dance with his hurley stick.

"It was a *tremendous* lot of work! Especially making up that stupid riddle. 'Tilling, willing, killing.' I spent an entire afternoon coming up with the rhymey bits."

The brat! I wanted to smack him with my hurley stick, but *no killing, no killing,* not to mention hitting him with my hurley would be a foul. "But Finnbar!" I sputtered. "Do you realize how much trouble you've caused?"

"Oh, but it was worth it," he crowed. "Don't you think? How often do I get to play at hurleys with my sister?"

My head started to hurt. My faery-brother Finnbar had set up this entire scenario because *he wanted me to play with him.*

"And it *was* funny watching the king eat!" he added. "And

the silly man making love to the frog! You must admit, you thought so too!"

When I get home, I thought, *if I ever get home, I am going to sit and play Barbies with Tammy till she screams for mercy.* In the meantime—

"You thought so too!" Finnbar laughed. "You thought so too!"

"Let the game begin!" King Conor bellowed.

It's just field hockey, i told myself, *as both teams* charged to gain possession of the sliothar. *With weird rules and magic people watching. You can do this. Just go with it.*

We managed to score some legitimate points during the first half of the game, but my team made two fouls, both committed by the captain, of course. First I ran five steps holding the sliothar, then I threw it instead of whacking it with my hand. Each one of those errors gave Queen Maeve's team a free strike and that tipped the advantage to their side, since Finnbar insisted on being his team's free-striker. Each time he conjured a golden eagle that aided his strike by catching the sliothar in its claws and carefully delivering it into the goal. Was this cheating? Maybe, but I wasn't going to be the one to argue with him.

Some of my teammates started grumbling for me to deliver some magic on the field as well (yeah, right), but instead I committed a third foul by shoulder-tackling Maeve a little too hard. We both ended up in the dirt.

"You bitch!" she said, in a friendly tone of admiration.

Fergus was by my side instantly. "Morganne, are you all right? Beloved, my beloved! Let me help you."

He lifted me to my feet and brushed the dirt off my clothes, leaving Maeve lying on the ground.

"Your boyfriend is cute," she said testily. "But he's no gentleman."

Of course, I thought to myself. *This is how it begins. It's me who introduces them.* "Fergus," I said, knowing full well what was about to happen. "This is a game, not a battle. Would you help Queen Maeve up, please?"

Fergus would do anything I asked, of course, and he extended his hand to the sprawled queen. She shamelessly checked him out, taking a long look up and down his shirtless, blue-painted, muscled warrior-dude bod. Then she grasped his hand firmly and pulled herself to her feet.

Chemistry. It zapped her, the minute they touched. I could see it on her face. Fergus didn't notice because he was still mooning over me, but if we won the game and the enchantments were broken his moonstruck condition would be cured quite soon. And guess who would be waiting in line?

"Your name." It was a question but she didn't say it like a question. She kept possession of Fergus's hand the way Cúchulainn kept possession of the sliothar. Like you'd have to lop off a limb to get it away from her.

"Fergus," he said gruffly. They were exactly the same height, and they stood nose to nose. "Fergus Mac Roy."

Maeve dropped Fergus's hand without a word and walked over to me.

"Mine," she said, right in my face.

"I know," I said.

It wasn't the answer she was expecting.

"foul!" yelled the referee. So far he'd been pretty fair, for an ogre.

"Morgan made another foul, so I get a free kick!" yelled Finnbar. "I'll do it I'll do it let me let me let me!"

Thanks to my fouls, Queen Maeve's team was three points ahead at the end of the first half. However, during my thirty cumulative minutes of hurling experience I had made some progress in my ability to run while balancing the sliothar on my hurley, and I felt confident I could avoid committing any more damaging fouls in the second half.

During halftime the merrows provided all the players with cool, refreshing drinks of water. It was the most delicious and thirst-quenching water I'd ever tasted. Salty and sweet at the same time, like magic Gatorade.

Fergus's knees and forearms were scraped and bleeding from diving to block goals. He seemed very happy. I knew I had to talk to him now, while I had the chance.

"Fergus," I said. "When the game is over—"

"I'll still love you, Morganne."

"That's nice, Fergus." I tried not to be distracted by how cute he looked with dirt on his face. "But if we win, when the game ends, so will the enchantments."

"It doesn't matter," he said, chugging his merrow drink. "I'll always feel the same way."

"Everybody thinks that when they're in love with someone. But you can—" I felt my mother's words coming out of my mouth, always a frightening experience. "—you can *move on*. And you will. And it's usually for the best."

"I'll always love you, Morganne." He moved to kiss me. I wondered if Maeve was watching. I stopped him.

"Listen, Fergus, please. I don't know what will happen to me when the game ends, and just in case we don't get to say good-bye—I wanted to thank you."

"For what?"

I tried to memorize the color of his eyes, a cornflower blue that sparkled in the light. If I ever forgot I'd just have to look at Colin.

"For loving me so truly," I said. "For treating me so well."

"But, Morganne." He touched my hair and tenderly pushed it away from my face. "There is no other way to love."

"You're right," I said. "And I promise you that I will always remember that from now on. Okay?"

He laughed. "Okay!" he said. It sounded so funny coming out of his mouth. "Okay, my captain!"

"Now let's win this game!" I hollered, loud enough for the whole stadium to hear me. "Let's win one for King Conor and Queen Dana!"

Ten thousand magical beings started doing the wave in the stands.

hurling was a fast and brutal sport. Unless the sliothar went out of bounds or a foul was called, the play was relentless, with both teams running back and forth across the long grassy field without relief, fighting over possession of the sliothar (which was no bigger than a baseball and easy to lose sight of) and trying to score a goal.

By the time we got to the final minutes, I was beyond winded. Fergus defended our goal like a crazed animal, and Cúchulainn just kept getting stronger and stronger. Like me he'd committed a personal foul (he'd whacked one of Queen Maeve's players on the thigh with his hurley in a fit of temper; luckily nothing important was lopped off), but it was largely thanks to Cúchulainn's ferocity that the score was now tied.

Finnbar, naturally, kept conjuring up flying carpets and enchanted surfboards and other faery-powered means to transport him swiftly back and forth across the field. The kid was barely sweating.

"Final play!" announced the ogre referee, after consulting his sundial. "Next point wins the game!"

The ref tossed the sliothar onto the field and it rolled right toward me. I scooped it up with my hurley and ran hard toward the goal. My defensive line fell back behind me and Cúchulainn raced ahead, whooping and showering the field with sparks.

"Isn't this fun!" yelled Finnbar. He was galloping after me on a silver-horned stag and swung his hurley hard against mine, knocking the sliothar into the air.

I leapt up and smacked the ball with my hand. "Pass!" I screamed, hoping Cúchulainn was in position.

He was, but just as he was reaching for the sliothar Queen Maeve intercepted. With a blood-curdling warrior cry, she expertly maneuevered the sliothar back across the field, punting it along the ground with her hurley stick just like in field hockey, scooping it up to safety when Cúchulainn was ready to steal it away, bouncing it up into her hand for a few strides and then back to the hurley—my defensive line was swarming around her like bees but no one could get the sliothar away from her.

She was barely close enough to the goal to attempt a shot, but Maeve was going for the gold anyway. "Score!" she screamed, and with a mighty swing she sent the sliothar sailing like a major league fastball, right at Fergus.

It was moving almost too fast to see, but Fergus jumped, stretched, reached, and—ouch!—caught it in his bare hand.

"Fek!" he shrieked in agony. But he didn't let go.

The crowd went insane. Fireworks made of fairy dust started to explode in the sky above us, spelling out FERGUS MAC ROY and providing an instant slo-mo replay of his amazing catch.

With a groan, Fergus tossed the sliothar sideways to Cúchulainn. Cúchulainn trapped it with his hurley and started to travel with it back toward the opposing goal. I could tell by the furious tornado spinning above his head that he was not going to surrender the sliothar to anyone, for any reason.

"No killing!" I yelled, as a precaution, but I knew my words didn't matter.

"I'll stop him!" It was Finnbar. He was all alone at the far end of the field, defending his goal against Cúchulainn. A little boy trying to block the approach of a freight train that had no brakes.

Where was his team? I wheeled around, looking for red-painted faces. I found them soon enough. They were dangling

helplessly in midair, ten feet above the center line, and looking very angry indeed, especially Maeve, whose salty protests
were certainly not fit for the ears of children.

"Nice work, Captain!" shouted King Conor from the
stands. But it was Finnbar's magic that had put his teammates
out of commission, not mine. Talk about hogging the ball!

"Let them go, Finnbar," I said. "You need your team!"

"But I want to do it myself!" he cried.

Cúchulainn was barreling single-mindedly toward the
goal. He was in full battle fury now, sparks flying, and there
was no stopping him. Finnbar was seconds away from being
flattened.

"And I don't want my brother to get hurt!" I yelled back.
True, Finnbar was a spoiled brat, but except for the magic
powers and immortality he was basically just a kid, right?

"Do you mean it?"

"Sure," I yelled. "You're the only brother I have." I winked
at him. He laughed, and in that moment he seemed exactly
like a normal little boy. Then Cúchulainn fired his shot.

It was a doozy, whipping through the air at ninety miles
an hour at least—till Finnbar pointed a finger. The sliothar
froze in the air and hung there for a moment before continu-
ing on its way, spinning and tumbling toward the goal in ex-
quisitely slow motion.

Foiled by magic! I saw Cúchulainn's rage rise in him and
pour out of his eyes like streams of molten lava. The odds of
us winning or getting out of this game without any killing
seemed to dwindle to zero, as the sliothar made its lazy, slow
arc toward the goal. Anybody could have caught it.

But Finnbar did nothing to stop the sliothar. Nothing at

all. We stood there, dumbstruck, as he happily watched it rotating against the sky, sailing in a long curved arc until it floated gently through the goalposts.

No one dared cheer.

"Beautiful shot!" Finnbar cried, breaking the silence. "I just wanted to see how it flew!"

"Game!" yelled the ogres, as the rest of Maeve's team dropped to the ground with a thud. "The victory goes to King Conor's team! Hip hip! Hurrah! Hip hip! Hurrah!"

the spectators charged the field, and it was the happiest kind of pandemonium.

Where was Fergus? I turned around, searching. King Conor and his wife were engaged in a public display of royal affection. The king suddenly looked twenty pounds lighter and was very handsome indeed, as if the weight from all that enchanted eating had melted away with the spell.

Nearby I overheard Erin speaking to Finnbar firmly. "Apology accepted. And as long as you behave like a gentleman, I will enjoy playing with you. But no more tricks."

"I promise," he said, sounding quite contrite.

Suddenly I was flying. Fergus had found me and lifted me up in a dizzying victory twirl.

"You did it!" he said. "You did it! Victorious captain!"

"Is the enchantment broken?" I searched his face, wanting to see the change for myself.

"It is." He smiled at me, his bright blue eyes twinkling with love. "I'm my own man once more. But still yours. Ever yours, Morganne."

I felt a little pang, thinking how Maeve would soon get to know Fergus in a way I hadn't. His handsome, dirty face started to go out of focus.

Their love would become the stuff of legend. Pretty cool, that. Something to aspire to, even.

There was so much to say, but everything was beginning to blur around the edges. "Good-bye!" I called, as Fergus picked me up again. My long hair whirled like streamers, making golden-red circles around us as we turned. "Don't wait for me, okay? Have a good life. I don't know when I'll be b—"

twenty-one

Cornflower-blue eyes in a freshly-shaven face, magic lips curved into a smile that was so very familiar.

"Colin!" I threw my arms around his neck and started to cry.

"There, there now, Mor! What's burst the plumbing all of a sudden?"

The clean aftershave smell of a modern man was like catnip. I buried my face in Colin's neck and made a wish that I could hide there forever.

I was back. I was Morgan. My hair was gone and I was in a strange bed, wearing a man's sweatshirt and tucked under two layers of twenty-first-century thermal polyester fleece blankets. I was freezing and my teeth were chattering.

And Colin was sitting on the edge of the bed, warm and damp and naked except for a towel, which he was finding hard to keep wrapped around his waist with me hanging on to him.

"Easy, there," he said, grabbing the towel as it nearly slipped off. "Let me at least get me Y-fronts on so we can converse like civilized people, eh?"

Forever in the neck plan canceled, for now. I let go of Colin and looked around. We were in a small Ye Olde Quaint Irish Inn–type bedroom that—as far as I knew—I'd never seen before.

"This whole time I've been in the shower and you're still shivering!" Colin said, sounding alarmed. "I'm bringing you some soup and that's that. You stay here and do as you're told. I shouldna have let you stay in the water so long; you've caught a chill right to the bone. And then driving back in your wet clothes, tsk! What a madcap pair we are, eh?" He held his towel on with one hand and rummaged through the bureau drawer with the other.

"If Patty finds you here in my room, yer man'll be looking for work by morning," he said, tossing his clothes everywhere. "But you were shivering and shaking and mumbling the whole drive back from the beach. I didn't want to leave you alone till you started acting sensible. How are you feeling now?"

We just got back from the beach? Brand new tears started running down my cheeks. Was I happy? Sad? Feelings are not so easy to label sometimes.

"What's the matter, Mor? Are you all right?" He looked so sweet and unself-conscious, standing there in his bare feet. "You're not upset about what happened tonight, are ye? We had a bit of a moment there, you and me, but all's well now; I was never really mad at ye, how could I be. . . ."

We just got back from the beach. My Long-ago adventure had taken, what? An hour? Two? The time-space continuum works in strange and mysterious ways.

"I got scared." I sniffed, knowing he wouldn't understand. "That I was gone too long."

He grinned. "Well, ye did stay underwater long enough to give your ol' pal Colin the devil's own scare! How was I to know ye've got lungs of iron?"

He prattled on about Jacques Cousteau and some woman who'd swum the Irish Sea, but I felt more like the guy in the Christmas movie who helps the angel get his wings. Or the old guy in the other Christmas movie who's stingy and mean and gets his ass whipped by a bunch of ghosts, but still wakes up in time to buy a Christmas turkey for his gimpy kid friend, Tiny Tim.

Goddess bless us, every one. And speaking of gimpy, Colin was becoming a hilarious sight standing there in a towel, clutching a pair of tighty-whities and staring at me like I was the one who looked like a nut.

"What an expression ye've got on your mug! What on earth are you brooding about, lass?"

"Christmas," I said, laughing and crying harder. I wiped my nose on the back of my hand, and it never once occurred to me that he would think I was gross. "I'm glad I didn't miss it."

"It's July, Morgan," he said patiently, searching for a matching sock. "Nobody's missing Christmas at the moment."

"It's just that I've been homesick," I said, trying to explain.

"For your ma and da?"

"No." I shook my head. "For here."

"Ah," he said. He walked over and sat on the bed next to me again. "That I understand. But you'll be back, never fear." Colin wrapped me tighter in the blankets, speaking softly in my ear. "Ireland is like that for some people—it gets in your blood and you can't stay away for long. Now keep still till I come back with the soup."

"You should put some clothes on first," I said.

"Right-o." He grabbed a pair of pants and ran back into the bathroom.

I rubbed my head. It felt so weird not having any hair. But it would grow back.

Me, in my padded bike shorts, standing on a huge stone slab with Lucia and Carrie.

Me, Heidi, Johannes, Sophie and Derek, in a giggling human pyramid near the door of an old stone castle.

Me, again, upside down, holding my bike and scowling at the camera as a cute little sheep waved its feet in the air.

"Whoops! Slide's in cockeyed, hold on." Patty took the slide out and squinted at it in the light.

"I keep telling you, a digital camera and a laptop running PowerPoint would do a much better job of this, Patty," Colin grumbled.

"You and your techno gadgets!" she scolded amiably, as she popped the slide back in the carousel.

All better now—I was standing on the ground, grinning, and the sheep was sniffing at my feet.

I hadn't missed Christmas, and I hadn't missed the bike tour either. By the time the week was over it was like I'd gotten two Irish vacations for the price of one. What a bargain! My dad would be pleased, if he ever knew.

The photos Patty showed us after dinner on our last night together made it easy to remember all that had happened. This was the vacation I'd talk about when I got home and people asked me about my summer.

I had a great time in Ireland, I'd say. *I stood on a stone slab. I visited a castle.*

And if I closed my eyes, I could see other pictures as well:

Me, in long hair and a cream-colored princess dress, swimming after a mermaid to the bottom of the sea.

Me, dancing to the music of a harp and a flute and a drum, as Fergus laughs and throws me back in a low tango dip.

I got along great with my tour mates and my ass never got sore.

Me, talking to a horse; me, arguing with a queen; me, racing down a magic field holding a hurley stick while thousands of faeries looked on.

The scenery was beautiful, and there were friendly sheep floating upside down in the air everywhere we went.

Which were more true? The pictures on the screen or the pictures in my head? I thought of my family photo albums: Did I actually *remember* being that bald baby on the sheepskin, the chubby blond toddler in the frilly dress at the zoo clutching a stuffed penguin, the strawberry-haired girl napping with her infant sister? Or was it the photos I remembered, and my parents' stories about them that I'd heard a million times?

Answer: Who cares? It was me in the pictures and me in the stories, and between them both and my own memories I could put together a pretty good map of where'd I'd been and where I might be going. But who could I tell about my Long-ago adventures? I knew I wouldn't believe me if I told those stories to myself.

"We have a tradition, here at the Emerald Cycle Bike Tour Company," said Patty, in a tone of jolly warning. "We call it the Emerald Awards, and everybody wins one. They're all in good fun, remember, and we hope you'll be entertained." Patty took out her inevitable clipboard. "To Heidi: *The Woman of Many Tongues Award,* for her fearless assault on the English language."

Patty handed her a certificate. "Thank you! I am loving the English!" exclaimed Heidi. "And the Irish slang, it is a bloody fekkin' wonder!"

"Easy on the language, dear," Patty said. "To Johannes," she continued. "*The Tireless Steed Award,* for cheerfully providing horsy rides to the children even after a long day on the bike."

"Neigh!" whinnied Johannes, as Sophie and Derek clapped in delight. That neigh sounded awfully familiar.

"To Carrie Pippin: *The Golden Hoop Award,* in honor of her passion for—what does this say, Colin?"

"Bling." Colin rolled his eyes.

"That's not a word, is it?" asked Patty, puzzled.

"Aye, 'tis," said Colin, exasperated. "Just read it, Pat, before everyone realizes how out of touch ye are with the modern world."

"Fine then. In honor of her passion for 'bling.'" She handed Carrie her certificate.

"Did you see the Claddagh ring Stuart bought me?" Carrie

gushed. She held out her hand for all to admire. "Isn't it pretty? And it's so *Irish*!"

Everyone leaned close to admire the ring, but I already knew what it looked like—two hands clasped around a heart, with a crown on top.

"Just like on *Buffy*." Carrie sighed romantically. "God, I would have been great in that part."

"Which brings us to Stuart!" said Patty. "To him we bestow *The Best and Final Offer Award*. I think we've all learned something about—"

"Sorry, hold that thought—" Stuart said, raising a hand. "Got a call coming in." He held the BlackBerry to his ear.

"Hey-hey, Stevie!" he said. "This isn't a great time; can I call you—hello? Hello? Can you hear me? Ow!" A big spark exploded next to his ear and made him jump back.

"That Spielberg," he joked nervously, staring at the smoking carcass of his BlackBerry. "Always with the special effects."

"You'll be needing a new one of those, I reckon," Patty remarked. "To our dear Lucy Faraday: *The Happily Ever After Award*, because we know there is much joy awaiting you in life." Lucia's certificate came with a big hug from Patty. When she sat down again, I hugged her too.

"Although Mrs. Billingsley cannot be with us tonight due to her medical situation, in absentia we present her with *The Aching Gut Award*, for bravery under duress."

The Billingsley children laughed heartily at this and clutched their sides with dramatic groans.

I'd found a note from Mrs. Billingsley slipped under the door of my room this morning.

I cannot thank you enough for the way you've taken care of Sophie and Derek this week. What a wretched time for me to get colitis!

"A few more awards!" announced Patty. "To Mr. Billingsley: *The King of his Castle Award*, for gracefully managing a family under severe pressure, without resorting to violence, heh heh!"

But because you volunteered to help mind the children, their holiday was not ruined; in fact I'm quite sure they had a better time with you than they would have with their father and myself!

"To young Sophie: *The Disappearing Act Award*, for her superlative skills in games of hide-and-seek! We almost left you in Killarney, you little minx!"

Because of you, Mr. B. was able to take the most tender care of me during my illness (and I am quite remarkably on the mend, by the way; all the doctors say so).

"To Derek: *The Future Rugby Star Award!*"
"You've got a mean kick there, pal—keep practicing!" said Colin, giving Derek a friendly clap on the back.

I do believe the experience has strengthened our marriage, and for this we owe you further thanks. If you ever need a place to stay in London, we would be honored to have you as our guest.

Warmest regards,
Mrs. B.

"And last, but certainly not least. To Morgan." The room got quiet.

"*The Changeling Award,*" said Patty. " 'Tis an old Irish myth that the faeries will sometimes come and steal a sweet baby from its cradle, leaving a foul-tempered changeling in its place."

Colin buried his head in his hands and stamped his feet in frustration. "Oh, not the old Irish myths again, Patty!"

She shot him a look that could flame broil a Whopper. "Some say," she went on, "in order to be rid of a changeling, you must trick it into revealing its true age."

I had to cover my mouth to squelch a sudden fit of hysteria. Out of the corner of my eye I saw that Colin was in a similar state.

Patty ignored our bad manners. "However it happened, we salute Morgan for the changes she made this week. Frankly I wasn't too sure you wanted to be here at first." My face was turning purple from the effort not to laugh, and Colin's fingernails were digging into my jeans. "But after a rough start you became a wonderful playmate for the children, a kind and cheerful companion for Lucia, a patient English tutor for Heidi and Johannes—"

"She saved my *ass* by finding that earring!" added Carrie.

"And she's a wicked good dancer," added Colin. "Remember Durty Nellie's, nudge nudge, wink wink?"

Durty Nellie's was the one thing I really couldn't remember about this trip, but so what? Nobody remembers everything about themselves, anyway.

"I can say truly," Patty intoned, sounding very regal, "none of us would have had such an enjoyable trip without you."

"Particularly the children," said Mr. Billingsley warmly, as Patty handed me my award.

"Which reminds me!" Patty put away her clipboard and stood up straight, her formidable chest on queenly display. "Repeat customers get a ten-percent discount, so do call us again! There are so many wonderful parts of Ireland left to explore. The Burren, the Ring of Kerry, the Dingle Peninsula . . ."

"The Dingle is my favorite," Colin whispered to me. "And it's the closest bit of Ireland to Connecticut, so now I like it even more. You come back for that one, all right?"

"Dingle," I said. "I always liked that name."

twenty-two

the next morning Colin drove me to the airport, and he even sprung for the short-term car park so he could walk me inside.

Much too soon we arrived at the spot where I would proceed to the gate with all the ticketed passengers, and he had to stand there watching me go. The Leaving Point, they should have called it. He kissed me good-bye, but not the way we'd kissed on the beach. He pressed those magic lips against my cheek and let them linger there just long enough for us both to remember. Long enough to make a promise too.

"I have a wee present for you," he said.

"It better be wee," I said. "My carry-on already won't zip."

"Is it my fault you're a pack rat?" He grinned. "Here. Don't get your hopes up; it didn't cost me a penny."

It was a book, an old one. The corners were frayed and

there were deep creases in the spine. The letters on the cover were stamped, with only a few dull flecks left to show they'd once been embossed in gold.

"*The Magical Tales of Ireland,*" I read.

"That's the book my grandparents used to read to me from when I was a boy-o." He sounded embarrassed. "I thought you might enjoy it. You seem to have developed an interest in all that faery claptrap."

The book was heavy with the weight of being read a thousand times. "Colin—this is part of your childhood," I said. "You shouldn't give it away."

He shoved his hands in his pockets. "I want you to have it," he said sheepishly. "Hang onto it for me, anyway. Time to clear off the dusty shelves and make room for the new! I got a whole pile of books I'll be reading for school next year, UNIX programming and human interface design, virtual communities, viral marketing, all dry as dust."

"I love it," I said. "Thank you. I'll read it on the plane."

"Only if the film's a bust," he said, deadpan. "Anything from the eighties with Chevy Chase in it, you can feel free to skip. Bye luv."

With a wink and a tip of his imaginary hat, he was gone.

that Colin. he almost got me, but of course Aer Lingus didn't show movies from the eighties. The "in-flight entertainment" was a recent film that starred one of those stand-up comics from Comedy Central playing all the parts, most of them involving fake boobs and wigs and bad accents. I decided to skip it anyway.

The Magical Tales of Ireland. I turned the yellowed pages until I found the table of contents. "How Cúchulainn Got His Name," was one story. "The Enchantress Morganne, Protector of the Realm of Ulster," was another.

I put the book away. I'd read it later, but not now. For what could be more magical than to fly across the sea? To get on a plane and then off again, a world away and back in time from where you began?

Even with the difference between Greenwich Mean Time and Greenwich, Connecticut, time, my plane didn't arrive till late. My dad picked me up at the airport, and he and Mom were so overjoyed to see me you'd think I'd been gone for thousands of years.

Tammy was already asleep when I got home, but the next day at breakfast when the four of us were finally together (my dad even took the morning off from work in honor of my homecoming), my parents said they had something to show me. They were pretty excited about it.

"It's Riverdance!" Dad said, pushing the Arts section of the *Connecticut Post* in front of me. "The famous Irish dance troupe. They're performing in Stamford tonight. Would you like to go?"

I stared at the ad.

The dancers were in pairs. Each couple stood cheek to cheek, one set of arms extended, hands tightly clasped, bodies arched together in a deep, sexy dip.

Oh *fek*. Riverdance was doing the *tango*.

But then I looked at the photo of the tangoing Irish

dancers, and the more I stared at it the less strange it seemed, until finally it didn't seem strange at all.

"No thanks," I said, handing the paper back. "I was kinda planning to stay home and tell Tammy a bedtime story tonight."

"You *are*?" Tammy couldn't believe her luck. "What is it about? Is it a long one? Make it about a princess, please!"

"It's about a magic faery mermaid princess," I said, smiling at her. "With long, strawberry-blond hair and a very pretty dress. And she's brave and clever and has magic powers, only she doesn't know it at first."

"Yay!" said Tammy, bouncing around the room like a rubber ball. "Yay!"

I felt like saying it too, so I did.

"Yay!"

I was so glad to have someone to tell.

about the author

Maryrose Wood owns a pair of padded bike shorts but you will be hard-pressed to find a photograph of her wearing them. However, she always dons a helmet when riding her bike, and you should as well. Helmet-hair is no reason to take chances with your skull.

Maryrose wrote *Sex Kittens and Horn Dawgs Fall in Love,* which was hailed as "an uproarisously funny debut" by *ALA Booklist*. Other nice things have been said about Maryrose and her work; you can see for yourself by visiting www.maryrosewood.com.

She lives in New York with her two children and a feisty little redheaded dog.